CONTENTS

BLOOM

By
Sarah Blynne

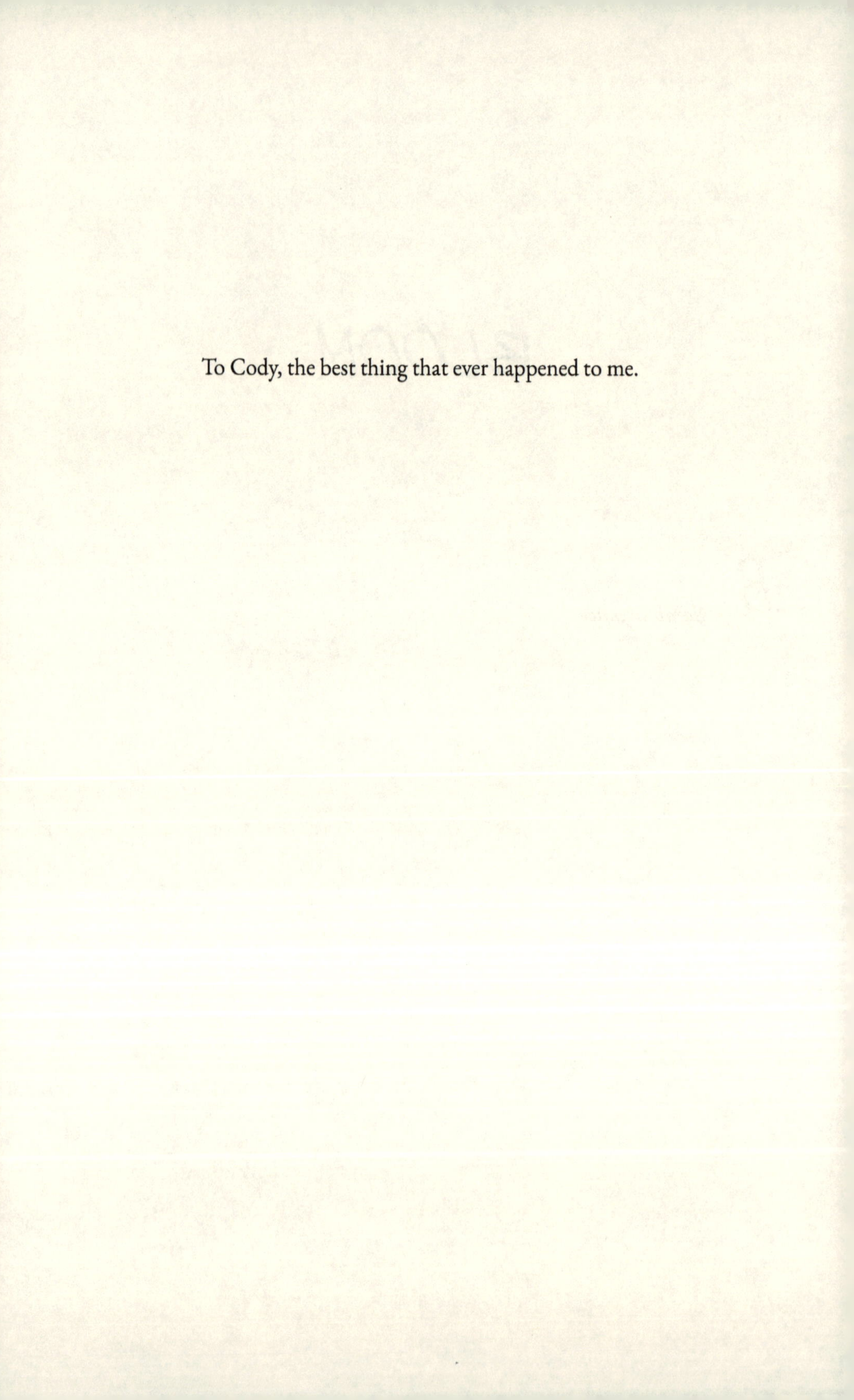

To Cody, the best thing that ever happened to me.

CHAPTER 1

"Well, Seth, it's not looking good," my 12th-grade counselor, Mr. Brian Nichol, says with a sigh. He frowns at me over his glasses, brows furrowed, and clearly passing judgment. I already know he doesn't like me, but I honestly can't blame him. I'm slouched down in a chair at a circular wooden desk, fingerless-gloved hands clasped behind my head, and looking down at my feet in Converse shoes. I reek of not giving a crap.

Because I don't.

I honestly haven't cared in the last couple of months.

Mr. Nichol turns to his computer screen. I peer over his salt-and-pepper head at his impeccable view of Commencement Bay. I have to admit, his office is in such a great spot; nearly half the walls of his office are glass windows, and each windowpane gives a beautiful view of the water. I can't help but admire it.

"It's only October, and your GPA is in the 1.0 range," Mr. Nichol continues. "But in the past, your GPA was between 3.5 and 3.8. What happened there?"

What happened, indeed?

Well, school has always been easy for me. Getting a high GPA in the past was no problem. I'm fully capable of acing all my classes. The problem is I just don't care anymore. I don't want to talk about the reasons why, and I don't want anyone to try to fix me, either. The only response I muster up is a shrug.

Mr. Nichol twists in his chair to face me. "Okay, well, you still have time to get back on track, though," he says with a glimmer of hope. "There's a couple of options. You can sign up for an athletic season to recover the credits –"

"Nope," I cut him off, shaking my head vehemently. Nothing sounds worse than being in sports. I firmly believe athletes get high from the torture of exercise.

"Okay, well, if you get a 1.0 this semester, then you must get a 2.0 next semester, and your first semester GPA will change to a 2.0. Then you can still graduate, and it will look better on your transcript when you apply for college."

A 2.0 is the lowest passing GPA a student can receive and still graduate. College isn't really on my radar anymore; otherwise, I would take this a lot more seriously. Up until recently, I did care about going to college. I had an idea of what classes I wanted to take and where to go. Those plans have flushed themselves down the toilet. It would be a miracle if I made my way back.

"But if you still refuse to do the work, and you get anything lower than 2.0, you'll have to repeat your senior year. Be a 'Super Senior,' as kids are calling it these days. I really don't want that for you, Seth."

"Super Senior" is an odd title, considering that it makes you sound better than you really are. As cool as being a "Super Senior" sounds, I don't want to be stuck here for another year. I don't want to disappoint my dad, but the work I'll have to do to get to where I need to be doesn't appeal to me. Mr. Nichol seems genuinely concerned, which I should appreciate. His concern would be better applied elsewhere, in my opinion.

"I'll think about it. Thank you," I nod at him as I grab my beat-up backpack off the ground.

"Wise choice, Seth," he replies with a grin and dismisses me with a wave. Outside Mr. Nichol's office, my redheaded best friend Mason O'Connell sits in the waiting area, texting on his flip phone.

"Finally, you're done!" he exclaims in triumph when he lifts up his head and pushes his glasses up his nose. "Let's get out of here and grab some food. I'm so hungry my stomach is eating itself." He stands up with his backpack, giving me a full view of his Spiderman T-shirt that I'm sure he's had since he was twelve. "What did he have to say that was so important that my stomach had to be put on hold?"

We make our way across the brick courtyard, walking over the golden S imprinted on the brick, surrounded by a large royal blue circle. This castle of a school is a historic landmark, so much so that it barely looks like a school from the outside. With the U-shaped building with spires on all the corners of the roof and planted gardens spotting the area, it makes for a postcard-worthy image.

"I'm failing all of my classes, and I can either be a Super Senior, take an athletic course, or actually put in the work."

"Are you really surprised?" Mason asks in an accusing tone. "Maybe you should actually try putting in the work."

"Maybe."

"Your loss, bro. But let's hurry up and get out of here." He pats me on the shoulder and walks in front of me as we cross the courtyard.

Mason is the definition of a geek, but he's extremely smart. He's a 4.0 student, a major video game nerd, and wants to go to college and get into Computer Science so he can get into the gaming world. Yeah, he has goals. You'd think I could learn from his determination. He and I met freshman year. We bonded over video games and *Family Guy* in Biology class. Normally, I live a reclusive life surrounded by acquaintances, but having Mason in my life is great. Besides my dad, he's my closest friend.

Mason follows me home to my small, two-story house on the corner of the street. The moment we enter the front door, Mason runs across our 70's style shag carpeting into the kitchen with yellowing linoleum and chipped countertops. Beyond the kitchen is the laundry and an office space that has turned into a storage unit.

"Pizza rolls, come to papa!" Mason hollers while grabbing the bag of pizza rolls from the freezer. Next to the kitchen, I go up the shag-carpeted stairs to my ultra-messy bedroom. Messy is an understatement. It looks like a tornado blew through here. The plastic blinds bent in a few different directions; collecting dust, just proves my point. On the opposite wall lays a spray-painted smiley face with X's as eyes, with its tongue sticking out. Apparently, spray painting a smiley face that appeared drunk or dead seemed funny to my friends and me.

I'm just glad my dad isn't home. The longer I can avoid talking to him about my conversation with Mr. Nichol, the better. I don't have it in me to explain why I chose not to participate in school.

I turn on my dual monitor computer that I'm sure lived with the dinosaurs, then take off my baggy gray zipper hoodie and sniff it to see if it needs washing. Definitely needs to be washed.

As my computer takes an eternity to load, I take my overflowing hamper and throw some clothes in the washer. I may be lazy when it comes to school or having goals, but I do care about my clothes smelling clean.

I load up *Family Guy* on YouTube when Mason comes in with a plate of piling pizza rolls and a bag of potato chips. "Good god, did you heat up the entire bag?" I ask.

He shrugs unapologetically, plopping into a beanbag chair. "My stomach nor I feel sorry," he smugly retorts.

We go to town on the mountain of fatty snacks and put on an episode of *Family Guy*. This has been our routine since we met. Normally, we would watch this on a regular TV, but I wanted to use the other monitor for writing on the Gaia Online forum. Writing used to be just a hobby, something that helped me get ideas on paper. Now, it's my lifeline. People – or avatars that represent actual people – seem to enjoy my work.

I open up my notebook and look at everything I wrote down. Since middle school, I had a system. I would write ideas down in a notebook, then come home and transfer them to a Gaia Online post or put them in a Microsoft Word document. It may seem like an odd system, but every writer has a way of doing things.

Mason peeks at my computer as I'm transferring my paper ideas into a post. "Why don't we get out your textbook and go over those assignments?" he says with a wave of his fist, adding a cheesy smile.

Just the idea of putting work into school makes my brain shrivel up into a raisin. "No thanks."

"Let's face it. You and I both know you don't want to be a Super Senior. What's it going to take for you to be motivated? Victor's just going to lecture you again."

My dad lectured me at the beginning of the year to get my act together so I could graduate, get into a decent college, and move forward in life. Don't get me wrong, I love my dad and value his opinion, but when it comes to him telling me to get my act together, it's harder for me to take his advice. Therapy has been his lifeline, as writing has been for me.

"I'll deal with it," I say, continuing to look between my notebook and computer screen.

Family Guy fills the quiet air and blends with the typing of my keys. Mason puts another pizza roll in his mouth, chewing pensively. "Just an idea," he starts. I get a sinking feeling in my stomach at what he's going to say. "Have you thought about...I don't know, getting a tutor?"

"I don't need a tutor."

"Then get a girlfriend." Mason wags his finger.

I spin around in my office chair, confusion clear in my expression. "A girlfriend? Where did that even come from?"

"I hear girlfriends can be a motivating factor."

"Or they can be a distraction," I counter.

"And how would that be any different from how you're living now?" Mason counters back.

"Fair point. But how do you know if a girl will motivate me?"

Mason's lips curve sheepishly, avoiding eye contact. "Just what I hear."

"Is that what Harmony does for you?" I ask. He's had a crush on an equally geeky girl named Harmony for a while now. Mason is too shy to tell her, though. He's kind of like me.

Here's the thing. Generally, I tend to live a reclusive life. Don't get me wrong, I like girls. I may keep to myself, but I do like girls. I've had crushes here and there.

The problem was I was always one of those people who observed from a distance but never took action. I never knew how to strike up a conversation with a girl out of nowhere. More specifically, a beautiful girl. It never felt comfortable going that route. I always waited for things to happen out of nowhere. Of course, it never did.

"We're not talking about me right now," he changes the subject. "I'm just exploring all options. I'm the loyal friend trying to avoid another discussion with your dad that I know for a fact you will complain about tomorrow."

"I'm not even interested in anyone," I take a pizza roll and turn back to my computer.

"There's the first problem," he points out mid-chew.

With a groan, I turn back to my computer and keep typing. By the time the *Family Guy* episode ends, I've managed to come up with a couple of paragraphs to post.

Mysterious Snowfield: Part 2

The man spotted a figure out in the distance. It wasn't a tree or an animal. No animal stood upright like this figure. He concluded that it was a human. He stepped closer with the grace of a stag, trudging through heavy amounts of snow to get a closer look.

A girl. A little girl. Probably around eleven years old. She doesn't move, though. Just standing there.

"Hello?" the man called out to her.

She didn't move, still as the snow on the ground.

In all honesty, I have no clue where this story is going. Ever since I started it, I wasn't sure how I wanted it to end. I just knew I wanted to keep people hanging with each post. Keep them interested.

I'm a good writer. I know I am. But it helps to have someone confirm that my story is going in a good direction. If only I had someone to collaborate with to help my stories flow better. Gaia Online is a great community, but I have yet to find someone to share ideas with.

Before I can post it, I hear a gentle knock on the door.

"You boys lookin' at naked chicks in there?" a deep, gruff voice asks behind my door.

"Oh boy, here we go," Mason says, leaning back in his chair and rolling his eyes.

I can't remember a time my dad didn't ask that question before opening any door I find myself on the other side of, even the bathroom. Apparently, being a guy in your teens and living a reclusive life means I must be obsessed with naked chicks. Regardless, he still thinks it's funny.

"No, Dad, we're not," I reply, exasperated. That's my response every single time, and yet he still wants to ask.

The sound of Dad entering my room blends with his deep chuckle. Victor Harris is the epitome of a blue-collar worker: scuffed-up boots, paint-stained jeans, an old shirt, and a big, strong body. He's grown out his beard a bit, and his gray hair is buried under an old baseball hat. I don't know where I got my extra curly brown hair, but it wasn't from him. I got my brown eyes from him for sure, though.

His demeanor changes the moment he sits at the edge of my unmade bed. He leans forward, taking his ball cap off. "I got a call from your Algebra teacher. You haven't been doin' your assignments, and you're already failin'. And I know that's not the only class you're failin'."

Crap. The one thing I wanted to keep from him ended up coming to light anyway.

"Okay, so this just got intense," Mason says uncomfortably. "I'll see myself out." Just as he leaves my bedroom, he turns and says to my dad, "To be fair, I did try getting him to do his homework. He's still being an idiot."

"Dude, get out of here." I wave at him with urgency.

"Or what?" Mason says with a taunting gleam in his eye.

"Or I'll tell Harmony about the birthmark on your butt."

"Okay, point taken, bye," he says hurriedly and runs down the hallway. Normally, I would find enjoyment in his scurrying off, but knowing I'm in trouble has dampened the mood.

Once Mason leaves, I find my dad eyeing me with disappointment and frustration. A look I really hate seeing glaring back at me. I slap my hands on my thighs and jump up from my chair. I need to escape, and quick. "I'm going to grab something to eat."

"Stop," he says with a stern roar as I'm close to the doorway. That tone always scared me as a kid, and it still scares me now. It's the don't-you-dare-pull-that-crap-on-me kind of tone, and it's one to take seriously. "Sit down."

Hanging my head, I turn around from the doorway and sit back down on the chair. "Before you started school," he begins. "I told you to work hard so you can graduate. The way it is right now, you're goin' to repeat your senior year. Is that what you really want? This is your *senior year*, Seth. You need to get your act together."

"I don't know what to tell you. I would rather write," I say. It's true. I express myself better in writing. Living in my character's story instead of living in my own reality, even for a short while, is my comfort, my biggest escape.

"Well, I'd rather go on a date with Cameron Diaz, but life don't work that way."

My face scrunches, questioning his taste in women. "Really, Dad? She smiles like the Joker."

"She's hot. Don't change the subject," he says firmly, then sighs heavily. "My point is that somethin' needs to change. You need somethin' that motivates you.

You need a goal. I've been learnin' that in therapy. You'd learn the same thing if you went with me."

"I'm not going to therapy with you, Dad." Voicing my feelings to a shrink who is legally obligated to judge me while being paid a butt ton of money is a hard no for me. He should already know that will be my answer. On the other hand, he doesn't try that hard to get me to go. He's okay with having a therapist to himself, and he's just attempting to play the part of an attentive dad. Either way, I'm not interested in opening up to anyone.

"Your loss. Even so, you need to do somethin'." Dad states with finality. "Let's try this. Pick a goal. Any goal. Maybe one that involves writin'. See if you can get one of your stories published in those books that have all those short stories." He snaps his fingers as he tries to think of the title. "Chicken something."

"*Chicken Soup for the Soul?*"

"Yeah, that one."

"Those are chick flicks in book form!" I argue. "I don't write those kinds of stories." Nor do I want to. I'd rather punch myself in the nuts. I'm a guy, for god's sake.

"Okay, then look up some schools with creative writin' courses. I want you to pick one that interests you and look at the requirements to get into that school. Start with that," he demands.

I respond with another shrug. Yes, I shrug a lot.I hear a *pop* from my Instant Messenger (a.k.a. IM for Instant Message) come through. I don't talk to a lot of people except Mason, so I only have one conclusion as to who is messaging me.

Debra*: Hi, honey. I really wish you would respond to me. I really miss you. Call me sometime.*

"Your mom still tryin' to talk to you?" Dad asks.

She messages me at least once a day. Sometimes, she'll even call me. After everything she put us through, she still has the gall to try to mend things with me. I want nothing to do with the woman that broke my dad's heart. *My* heart. Maybe I'm being petty, but seeing my dad so miserable has been hard to watch, and I fully blame her.

I close the message and twist in my chair to face Dad. "Don't keep holdin' onto that anger, son," he advises. "And don't let what happened be the excuse that you don't do better in life."

Easier said than done. The anger is still fresh. It's not something I can get over in a day. But if there's one thing I've learned from all this, it's that I want to be nothing like her.

"Okay. Get to it," Dad commands with a wave of his hand. He leaves my room and heads down the hall. I turn back to my computer to keep writing, relieved to be in my home space again.

Truth be told, I don't like letting my dad down. My life consists of just going through the motions. I go to school because I have to. I eat because I have to. I sleep because I have to. I wake up because I have to. The only thing that seems to keep me from sinking deeper into the endless cycle of routine is writing. Writing is the one thing that's outside the scope of routine. Each story is different. Each event in the story is different. I can choose how it ends. It keeps me distracted in a way that school hasn't.

"Oh, and pick somethin' close to home!" Dad shouts from the stairs. "And not some hotshot university like Yale! We're broke, and your old man ain't ready to be alone yet!"

I let out a chuckle. My poor dad. He may be going to therapy, but that doesn't make him any less afraid to be by himself. I wasn't planning to move out anytime soon, anyway. I have a feeling I'll be here keeping him company for a while.

As *Family Guy* plays on mute on one screen and my story is laid out in front of me on the other, I ponder my options. This would be a good time to do what my dad says and pick a goal—research schools with writing courses. I already know those schools will say I need a good GPA that I need to pass my classes, which requires me to put in the effort, which doesn't interest me. Thanks for nothing, Mom.

Instead, I turned back to my Gaia post and reread the excerpt of my story. Once I post it, I make one last ditch effort for collaboration with a separate post.

Wannabe_peter_griffin: *Looking for someone to help me with my story ideas. I need a good hook for the next segment of my story. If you read any of my posts, maybe you can help with the next step.*

Another *pop* from my Instant Messenger sounds on my computer. Praying that it's not my mom again, I open it.

Mason*: I swear if you tell Harmony about my birthmark, I will make you impotent.*

I burst into uproarious laughter, forgetting that I threatened to tell his crush about that. I only know about it because he would always change clothes in the locker room after everyone else left P.E. One day, I stayed behind because I kept wondering why my only friend was so private. After he screamed like a little girl when I caught him, he revealed his secret. I laughed because it's shaped like a heart. People laughing at him was what he was trying to avoid in the first place. He made me swear I would never tell. After three years, his secret has been safe with me.

Ignoring his message, I turn *Family Guy* back on in search of more uproarious laughs and a further escape from reality.

"Did you finish this book?" Mason takes a seat in the row next to me in English class and holds up *After the Rain* by Norma Fox Mazer in front of his Batman T-shirt. The one-minute bell goes off, and students quickly filter in like a school of fish. With six floors in this school, kids have to hustle during passing period.

I sit in my seat, chin resting on my hand, doodling in my notebook, being the epitome of an unprepared student.

"Only because I like getting to know other author's writing styles," I answer.

"Bull. You have a girly side," Mason accuses.

"I'm serious. Plus, I was bored."

"That's a more Seth-like answer," Mason points at me, then turns back to his desk. "God, I felt my privates shrivel up from reading this. So many girl problems. I had to play *Halo* just to feel masculine again."

That makes me laugh aloud. "That's because it does suck."

For an English assignment, we had to read a book about a teenager named Rachel who ended up taking care of her dying grandfather. Meanwhile, she worries about never experiencing her first kiss before she turns sixteen. The only reason I can relate to that part is that I've never had a girlfriend; therefore, I've never been kissed. I'm seventeen, and at that age, most guys have at least had their first kiss.

The bell rings to signal the start of class. Mrs. Stacy Buhler (pronounced "Bueller." As in Ferris Bueller. Yes, I laughed when I heard it the first time) stands in front of the classroom and enthusiastically goes into discussing the book. I, on the other hand, go into a trance when I look at a quote written on the whiteboard. Mrs. Buhler writes quotes from Shakespeare's work on that board every day, so this is nothing new. For some reason, I take the time to read this one.

We know what we are but know not what we may be.

What am I now? Lazy, basic, creative. What *could* I be? Hard to say. Mr. Nichol and my dad seem to think I have the potential to become better. To become something. Work my way to be an author. Maybe even a writing coach.

Yeah right. I'll more than likely end up working at McDonald's till my sixties.

"Seth." Mrs. Buhler's voice calls me out of my train of thought. She searches me from her thick-rimmed glasses. "Why do you think the author titled this book *After the Rain*?"

This is embarrassing. To be honest, though, I wondered the same thing. The book was about an emotional teenage girl, not about anything after rain falling. I also didn't care enough to think about it deeply.

"I don't know," I admit quietly enough that only Mrs. Buhler could hear.

Mrs. Buhler purses her lips and subtly nods, annoyed. "Remember, every title has some kind of connection to the story," she addresses the class, but clearly saying it for my benefit. "Sometimes we have to think outside the box, think deeper about the 'why' behind it. So let's talk about the overall theme of the story."

Mrs. Buhler goes on to talk, and then I hear the chair creaking next to me as Mason leans over to whisper, "Can we talk about not making us read books that make my privates shrivel up?"

I snort and pinch my lips together tightly to keep from busting up in laughter. Mrs. Buhler whips her gaze at us and gives us the death glare that warns us to keep quiet. Apparently, my snort gave us away. Once she's satisfied that we're looking only at her, she continues talking.

My eyes land on the girl sitting in front of Mason, also holding back laughter as she takes notes. First impression: she's studious. She also knows what's funny, which means she has a good sense of humor. From her profile, I only see dark blonde hair in a mid-ponytail, a Def Leppard t-shirt, jeans, and skater shoes propped on a metal bar connected to the desk. She's simple. I like simple. I live my life around it.

Mason suggested I get a girlfriend, but it won't solve all my problems. I don't have an interest in girls right now. I don't have an interest in much of anything anymore.

That's particularly true when I check the Gaia writing forum during Microsoft Academy class, the last class of the day. I'm extremely thankful that internet security sucks at this school. Line Rider was taking over for a while until that became blocked, but everything else is open for access. It's perfect for guys like me to do everything except what I'm supposed to do.

I've gotten quite a few comments on the last excerpt of my story, which include the usual "I can't wait to read more!" or "awesome job" or "this story is dope, dudebro."

"Dudebro" is a new one. At least I'm getting reader traffic. As long as that happens, people can call me anything they want.

After scrolling through more of the same type of comments, I go to my forum post. I'm shocked to find that one person actually left a comment.

Marvel_lunatic*: I'm so glad I found this post because I'm having the same problem. I'm trying to create my own comic series (somewhat Marvel-inspired), but*

I'm having trouble with the plot. Can someone help me? The people in the art forum told me I could find help here!

Marvel_lunatic. What a unique username. Whoever this is enjoys brainstorming plot ideas like I do. Based on the avatar, *marvel_lunatic* is a girl—a cute, goth-looking girl in mostly dark clothes and shoes. For the most part, avatars reflect the actual person's taste in dress and style. If this girl's avatar is goth style, she's probably a goth in real life. My avatar, on the other hand, is a fancy version of myself: straight brown hair, jeans, basketball shoes, a dress shirt, and a suit jacket. Do I actually dress like that? Not even close. My outfits consist of baggy thrift store finds, with black fingerless gloves tossed in for fun.

I stare at the comment thoughtfully. I needed a collaborator, and this person just gave me an open ticket. However, there might be a problem. I only know two things about Marvel. One, Spiderman is a Marvel superhero. Two, they make great movies. That's the extent of my knowledge. If that sends her running for the hills, I can at least say I tried.

Wannabe_peter_griffin: *I'll help you if you'll help me* ☺

While I wait for *marvel_lunatic*'s response, I pretend to do the class assignment for Microsoft Excel. I might as well make Mr. Niendorf think I'm being productive. Although I'm sure he's aware I'm failing this class as well.

A *pop* sound comes from my computer in the dead quiet of the classroom, and panic shoots up my spine from the noise. I turn down the volume, making sure I don't get caught. I sneak a peek at the old, lanky teacher to see if he heard me. As he stares at his desktop and clicks away, that's my cue that I'm in the clear.

I check my notifications on Gaia, and I see a reply to my comment.

Marvel_lunatic: *Great! I'll send you an IM.*

Oh, we're going straight to talking in private. Okay then. Directly messaging with strangers is new territory for me. Commenting on stranger's posts is a different story.

Before I can wait for *marvel_lunatic* to send me a direct message, the bell rings. I make a point to hurry to my car so I can race home and turn on my computer.

I really want to know what she needs help with, and I want to know how she can help with my own writing.

Once I get settled at my computer, I log back into Gaia to find a pending friend request. Since you can only send direct messages to people on your friends list, I accept the request. I'm not sure how long it's going to take her to send me a message, but I decide to scroll through more comments on my story as I wait.

Then I hear the *pop* of a private message notification. That didn't take long at all. This girl is serious. Works for me. A business relationship is all I really need here.

Marvel_lunatic: *Hi there! Ok, so I'm stuck on the plot of my comic series. I attached one of my drawings that I was thinking of using for the story, maybe to help you get an idea of what I'm going for. I was thinking the main character has to defeat this creature to save the world. I just don't know how she would go about doing that. Any ideas?*

The attachment opens to a drawing of a black, ugly creature with tentacles around its neck and red eyes, with dark gray clouds and a red sky. It looks as if she drew a roaring lion with its four legs and open jaw and fangs, then gave an extremely demented twist. It's not a pleasant creature, which I think was the goal.

This art...is incredible.

The clarity and detail are phenomenal. Reading her message, she seemed to have doubt in herself and her ability to create. I don't see it that way, though. This girl has a gift and serious potential. I don't hesitate to let her know of that.

Wannabe_peter_griffin: *Dear marvel_lunatic, wow! Your picture is absolutely amazing. I'm impressed. Good job! I do have to admit, though, I don't know much about Marvel, but I'll try to help where I can. What you have for the plot is a good starting point. To help narrow it down, ask yourself what this creature is doing to make your character need to save the world. Did it destroy her family/people, and she's seeking revenge? Did someone train this monster to hunt your character down? If so, why? Also, look at who you want your character to be and why she has to do this. Does that make sense? – wannabe_peter_griffin*

I don't want to tell her my name yet. Internet security and all.

Marvel_lunatic: Those are all really good ideas. That helps a lot, thank you so much! I've been stuck on that for a while. And for the record...how does one not know anything about Marvel? Lol

Wannabe_peter_griffin: Dear marvel_lunatic, glad I could help! As for Marvel...to be fair, I'm more of a Family Guy person, if you couldn't already tell by my username ☺ - wannabe_peter_griffin

Marvel_lunatic: I love Family Guy! One of my favorite shows.

A girl that loves *Family Guy*? Now, she's piqued my interest. As far as I know, it's usually guys that like that show because of its offensive humor. Seth MacFarlane is a comedic genius. It's even better that we share a first name.

Wannabe_peter_griffin: Dear marvel_lunatic, that's awesome! That show is my favorite pastime, and writing, of course. My dad always tells me he'd rather see me do homework than have to hear Peter Griffin's retarded voice, lol. - wannabe_peter_griffin

Marvel_lunatic: I'm with you. I hate homework. And school, lol! What grade are you in?

Just when I thought this conversation couldn't get any better, she says something like that. A girl after my own heart. Someone who understands my struggle. And she's fearlessly asking personal questions now. Shockingly, I'm cool with it.

Wannabe_peter_griffin: Dear marvel_lunatic, I'm a senior in high school. What about you? If I'm talking to a grade school girl, this could get very awkward. - wannabe_peter_griffin

Marvel_lunatic: Wow, what a coincidence! I'm a high school senior, too. Where are you from? By the way, you don't have to be so formal with me. I'm not a CEO or anything ☺

Wannabe_peter_griffin: Ok, I'll stop being so formal ☺ I hail from Stadium High School in Tacoma, WA. What about you? - wannabe_peter_griffin (my being formal is making a comeback here)

Marvel_lunatic: Hail? Are we in the medieval era? LOL! I go to Federal Way High School! What are the odds that we'd live in the same state, close to each other, and be the same age? Maybe it's fate! Oops, that sounded creepy. I hope I didn't creep you out. Did I creep you out? □

Her insecurity is endearing. She may have a point, though. Maybe it is fate. Mason might be on to something because it's been a lot of fun talking to her. For someone who doesn't have a lot of experience talking to girls, I feel like I'm doing a really good job here. I'm even impressing myself. Maybe I'm just more charming in writing than I am face-to-face.

Before I know it, it's dark outside. I didn't realize we had been chatting off and on for hours. I haven't even seen my dad today. However, sometimes, he has painting projects that keep him out late.

I sigh heavily at the fact that I have to go to bed and live my routine life all over again. All I want to do is talk to this mystery girl. Keep escaping my reality in a way that doesn't involve responsibility. The last thing I want to do is relive another monotonous day, but I don't have much of a choice.

Wannabe_peter_griffin: *Not creeped out at all. I hate to do this, but I need to log off. Nice talking to you…(insert name here if you feel comfortable telling me)*

Marvel_lunatic: *I'm such an idiot, I didn't even introduce myself. I'm Tessa. Nice to meet you…I didn't get your name either. I'm so bad at this. Haha!*

Wannabe_peter_griffin: *I'm Seth. If you want to talk more, my email is wannabepetergriffin@yahoo.com. I had fun chatting with you* ☺ *talk soon?*

I mentally pat myself on the back for being bold enough to give her my contact information. No phone number. Seems too intimate to share that right away.

Marvel_lunatic: *Wow, thank you, Seth! I'll send you some more artwork. You should send me some of your work as well. Might help my creativity a bit too. I appreciate your help again. I'll talk to you tomorrow* ☺

We had veered way off the writing topic that I totally forgot that was what started this conversation in the first place. As I get ready for bed, needing help with my story is the last thing on my mind.

CHAPTER 2

*S*eth,

I just finished your Snowfield story from the beginning to the last post you did, and I can't wait to see what you're going to write next! I think what you should write next is something that no one saw coming. Maybe she was a plant to lead your character to something dangerous. Maybe she was the product of a bad science experiment. Just an idea! Those might sound stupid, but it's the first thing that came to mind.

*I attached another drawing that I had worked on. Working on the hero of my story now. Hope you like it! *cringe**

As for my favorite snack. Popcorn. Always popcorn. Particularly movie theater popcorn, but if I'm desperate, Orville Redenbacher has my back. What about you? - Tessa

Dear Tessa,

Thank you for your ideas. I'll see what I come up with! Your art is amazing, as always. You have a gift. She looks like she's about to dominate the world with her black costume. This could easily be a movie poster!

No one can do popcorn like movie theaters. I'd have to say pizza rolls are my favorite snack. Mason and I eat them like ravenous bears after school most of the time. My dad can barely keep up with us. – Seth

Seth,

Why do teenage boys eat like it's the last meal they'll ever have? I swear, they're all pigs! – Tessa

Dear Tessa,

*I'm going to skip over the fact that you basically called me a pig and point out that you are right *wink*. Mason eats a mountain of pizza rolls every time he comes over, and I never understand how he stays skinny. – Seth*

Seth,

I always envy guys. They can stay skinny and eat everything they want, yet if I do that, I'll look like an Oompa Loompa. – Tessa

Dear Tessa,

*Yes, the world is quite an unfair place. I demand we protest! *forcefully thumping my desk with my fist* – Seth*

Seth,

Ah yes, that will solve all the world's problems, protesting that we change the un-fairness of women gaining weight. – Tessa

Dear Tessa,

I sense a lot of sarcasm in your email. I'm offended. – Seth

Seth,

I'm so sorry. I was totally kidding! Just going along with your jokes! Don't hate me :(- Tessa

Dear Tessa,

I was totally kidding. I don't get offended easily. I mean, you're talking to someone who watches Family Guy ☺ tone gets lost in emails.

Sitting in Microsoft Academy class, I think about how to conclude this email, smiling like a giddy teenager. Yes, I decided to go back to being formal. I can't help myself.

Emailing Tessa over the last few days has been, dare I say, a lot of fun. Now that I have someone else emailing me, I actually look forward to checking my email and not seeing one from my mom. So, yes, I've concluded that I'm interested in Tessa. I never expected to form a romantic attachment and a virtual one at that. It's a foreign feeling to me, considering it's been since seventh grade since I had a crush on someone.

I liked a girl named Britney. She was a super cute, flirty blonde-haired girl, and she had the biggest boobs I'd ever seen. As in, they could easily smack her in the face when she ran; that's how big they were. One time, I actually tried to talk to her, but when she said, "Eyes up here, creep", I knew she caught me staring at her chest, and she did everything she could to avoid me. She ended up going out with a guy who wore a chain necklace and an entire bottle of cologne. I stopped trying after that.

Mr. Niendorf clasps his hands behind his back and wanders around the room to make sure students are doing their assignments. My grade speaks for itself, but I don't want to show my lack of focus too much either, so I open up Microsoft Excel. I don't even know if we're supposed to be on Excel.

The old fart glances at my screen and keeps going. I stare at the open worksheet, pretending to think about what I'm doing. If I'm thinking about anything, it's the fact that I seem to be really good at pretending to be busy.

Once he's out of sight, I reopen my email and ponder over my exchange with Tessa since we met. The only contact we've had has been through email. I'd be lying if I said I didn't want to hear her voice. Or meet her face-to-face, for that matter. Talking on the phone seems like a big step. There's no label on whatever this is, but I would like to explore if it's just friendship or if it has the potential to be something more.

To my own surprise, I want the latter. For the first time since middle school, I want to know what it's like to hold someone's hand. I want to show affection. I want someone to be loyal to and prove to her that I am not a selfish person.

I want a girlfriend.

Fingers hovering over the keyboard, I give myself one chance to back out of what I'm about to do. That chance comes and goes, though, when I finish my email to Tessa.

So, I was thinking we could talk on the phone sometime. If you don't want to, it's okay, I just wanted to leave it out there just in case. 555-1969 – Seth

I take a deep breath and send the email, wondering if she will take me up on my offer. When the bell rings, I book it out of the classroom and up the steps to the courtyard. Each step I take, my heart races with the thought of talking on the phone...with a girl. When we first started talking, she showed a hint of anxiety in her messages, especially when she thought she scared me off.

"Seth!" Mason comes up from behind me and climbs onto my back. I stop, and he slides off. "I feel like I haven't seen you in a million years. What's going on?"

"It's only been a couple of days," I say while speed-walking away from him. I haven't told him about Tessa yet. I didn't think there was anything to tell since I don't even know what we are.

"Oh my god," a Cheshire cat grin spreads on his face, footsteps catching up to me. "It's a girl, isn't it? You've got a crush on someone."

"I don't know what you're talking about," I lift my chin in defiance.

"Uh-huh. You're full of crap. It's okay, I get it." He waves me off. "I don't need you. I'll just immerse myself in ice cream and *Halo* while I cry over your infidelity."

"I can actually see you doing that."

"Screw you." Mason pushes my shoulder. "You go home and talk to your girlfriend, who you won't admit is your girlfriend, but she's totally your girlfriend."

"Okay, bye," I say quickly and descend the steps to the parking garage.

"Just from that, I know you got a girlfriend!" Mason calls to me. "Traitor!"

I bark out a laugh and practically hurry to my car. By the time I got home and checked my email, she still hadn't responded. My heart collapses to the pit of my stomach. She usually responds within minutes. Maybe I'm the one that scared her off this time. Maybe I caught her off guard. Heck, I even caught myself off guard by giving her my number. This girl has me in all sorts of scrambled thoughts.

To distract myself, I put *Family Guy* on YouTube and chow down on a quesadilla I made. This is the definition of bachelor life right here, taking a break from pizza rolls and eating the most basic thing I can make.

I really should be listening to Dad's advice and looking into schools. My head and heart are not on the same page, and motivation is nonexistent. We as humans are naturally compelled to give our time and energy to things that matter to us, while everything else gets pushed to the back burner.

My flip phone vibrates loudly on my desk, causing me to jump in surprise. The number on the screen doesn't look familiar, but the area code is local.

I flip open my phone. "Hello?" I answer in an irritated and bored manner.

Silence. Freaking telemarketers. What a waste of time. I pull my phone away from my ear to hang up, then –

"Hey, Seth?" a sweet, feminine voice finally says.

I bring the phone back to my ear. "Yeah?"

"Hey. It's Tessa."

Holy crap! She actually called me. That's just what I was hoping would happen. A flood of pent-up excitement bursts through me, which then turns into panic. I haven't talked to a girl on the phone in...well, ever. I'm dealing with a crush for the first time in years. My brain can't seem to understand that I don't have to be a bumbling idiot around a crush.

Now, it's been a good ten seconds since I've said anything.

"Hello? Did I lose you?" Tessa's sweet voice fills my ears again. Oh, right. I need to say something.

I clear my throat. "Oh. Yeah. Hey. So. How're they hanging?" I blurt out.

You are such an idiot. What does that even mean?

"What?"

Valid question. She doesn't sound weirded out, but more like she's trying not to laugh. Now we know that whatever charm I possessed behind a screen is long gone when it comes to phone conversations.

"Never mind." I shake my head. "I'll start over. Hi."

"Did I call at a bad time?" she asks sweetly. We've never shared any photos of ourselves since we started talking, so I can't put a face to the voice, but she seems adorable.

"No, not at all. What's up?" My heart is doing major cardio in my chest. I have no idea if I've scored any points with this girl, and it's making me nervous. I don't remember the last time I cared this much about what a girl thought of me.

"Well, you gave me your number," she says while stumbling over her words, "and I, uh, well, I feel comfortable enough talking to you over email, so I thought, why not try calling him? Besides, I wanted to know what your voice sounded like."

She's clearly nervous, as am I. Yet, we were on the exact same page as far as hearing each other's voices, and she was brave enough to call me. She easily could have rejected my offer. Suddenly, the instinct to put her at ease kicks in. As she said, we talk like we're good friends over email. This shouldn't be any different.

"Right. That's cool. That's good. Good for you," I ramble. I cover the mike of my phone and chastise myself. The first step of making someone feel at ease. I need to stop sounding like a rambling idiot.

"Yeah," she giggles. Then, the awkward silence reappears. There goes my charm. Wore off as if someone took a cloth and wiped it out of my abilities.

Tessa clears her throat. "So I've been working on a drawing for your *Mysterious Snowfield* story."

"Oh really? Taking a break from your comic?"

"For now," she says sheepishly. "Your story got me inspired. But I can't decide what material I would use, acrylic or watercolor or airbrush. Or even Adobe Illustrator. Then, I would have to decide whether to use an illustration board or canvas. Or what colors I can use that shows the overall feel of the story." She pauses and takes a breath. "If you can't already tell, I ramble when I'm nervous."

It helps that she's as nervous as I am. Okay, it's time to put her at ease.

I can do this.

I can have a normal conversation.

"Don't worry about it, and thank you. I really like the artwork you've been showing me, too."

"Really? I always worry it's the kind of art that's been done before. But everyone seems to have their own style, and artists are told to have their own style. This is mine, so…" she says with uncertainty. Tessa definitely is a chatty girl, and someone like me may find it annoying, but for some reason, it's endearing to me.

"I wouldn't worry about that," I tell her, putting her at ease. "If that's your niche and it works for you, then people will like it."

"That's a funny word," Tessa giggles. I could have a recording of her giggle on repeat, and I wouldn't get tired of it. "Niche. Is it neesh? Or nish?"

"I have no idea," I chuckle in response, and she laughs with me.

"You actually have a really deep voice. I like it," she says with a flirtatious tone. She's eased up a little bit. This is good, I'm doing something right.

"Why thank you," I respond in a much lower octave. It makes her laugh harder, and I feel myself relaxing. I even find myself smiling. Too bad she can't see the effect she's having on me.

Before I know it, we're talking about voices and singing. I mostly listen to her ramble, but I don't care. I never expected this turn of events to happen so quickly. This is so out of my routine that I almost don't know what to do with myself. Maybe this is what my dad was talking about. Maybe this is the perfect opportunity to find something that makes me happy and motivates me. Mason also suggested I find a girlfriend, so maybe this is the start of some positive changes. I have no idea if it'll help with anything that's upside down in my life, so I'm somewhat reluctant.

I won't know unless I try it.

"So, my phone is about to die; I'll have to go soon," I tell her to conclude the conversation and do the second most unthinkable thing of the day. My heartbeat clogs my vocal cords knowing that I am about to take a leap for the first time in my life. "Listen. I would like to, you know, meet up sometime. Would that be okay?"

There's a pause on the other line, but I swear I can hear her smile. "I would like that," she says cheerfully.

Mason: I knew *you* had a girlfriend.

Seth: For god's sake, she is not my girlfriend. I'm meeting her for the first time on Saturday. We've been talking, but that does not mean she's my girlfriend.

Seth: I knew I would regret telling you about her.

Mason: Yeah, yeah, keep telling yourself that, Casanova. It's going to happen soon enough. She'll take up all your time, and our Family Guy extravaganzas will be a thing of the past. Ice cream will be my new best friend, then I'll get fat, then Harmony won't even look in my direction, and I'll die a lonely man.

Seth:...

Seth: I have no words.

Mason: You know it's true. You'll have no one to blame but yourself for my impending obesity.

Seth: I'm not going to take responsibility for that.

Mason: You should.

Seth: You're so gay.

Mason: I love you too. You know, if I had known you were such a stud muffin, I would've asked you for girl advice a long time ago.

Seth: That's what the Internet is for.

Mason: Did you have to look up what to do on a date?

Seth:...No.

Mason: You sit on a throne of lies.

Seth: Quoting "Elf" doesn't make you sound original. That's my tip for the day.

Mason: Your tip had nothing to do with girls, though. Your Internet searching has proved you useless.

Seth: Glad I could be of service.

Mason: Let me know how it goes. Bye, stud muffin. *blows kiss*

Seth: I hate you.

CHAPTER 3

Clearly, one phone conversation with Tessa wasn't enough practice because I'm waiting for Tessa at Starbucks on Saturday afternoon, my heart racing a mile a minute. I didn't even dress up that nice; that's how bad I am at this. I even had a hard time picking a seat, whether to sit in the middle of the seating area or by the window to get some warmth from the sunlight. I chose the window. My gaze whips back from the window to the entrance every few seconds to see if she's arrived yet.

Finally, a teen girl enters, dressed up in black combat boots and cargo pants, a black hoodie with Spiderman on it, and a Spiderman beanie. Considering that she is aware that I only know a little about Spiderman, and she loves Marvel comics, I know the girl standing on the other side of the shop is Tessa Copeland.

Tessa spots me by the window and makes her way over to me. My heartbeat races more with each step she takes, to the point where I'm sure it'll burst from my chest at any moment. She's as cute as I imagined. Scratch that, she's *beautiful*. It will be a miracle if I get through this without passing out.

She sweeps her dark brown hair away from her eyes. "Hi. Seth, right?" she inquires with a hint of a smile, showing her crooked incisor.

I finally manage to feel my legs again when I stand. "Yeah," I choke out.

"Hi, I'm Tessa," she holds out a fingerless gloved hand, each fingernail coated in black nail polish. This girl really likes black, I guess—a perfect reflection of her Gaia Online avatar.

"Hi, nice to meet you, I'm Seth." I shake her hand. "Wait, you already knew that," I hang my head in defeat.

I pull out her chair for her because Google says that's what women like for guys to do. Yes, I had to research what women like; I just didn't want to admit it to Mason.

"Yeah, nice to meet you too!" she chirps while she takes off her hoodie to drape it over her chair, not even acknowledging that I just made a gentlemanly move. Before I knew it, her hands were flying everywhere, and she was talking quickly. I sit back in my chair and rest my chin on my hand. "I'm relieved that you look just like you described. Not that I thought you were lying, but I've read a lot of nightmare stories about people meeting online thinking they'll look meet the person they're looking for, but they look nothing like they say and –"

She freezes when she sees me sitting there, listening to her talk. "Shoot, I'm rambling again. I'm boring you, aren't I?" She laughs nervously and plants her hands to her sides.

I didn't mind it. I was just going with the flow. "Not at all," I reply with a shake of my head, still gazing at the beautiful creature in front of me.

Tessa blushes and breaks eye contact, hands clasped in front of her. Two nervous people are not a good combination, and I need to break the tension. I gesture to the counter. "Well, we're here. Let's get a drink."

We get up from the table and step up to the register. I let her go in front of me to the counter to admire her petite, thin body hiding in baggy clothes.

"Hey, Tessa," the male barista says with a charming smile. Immediately, I sensed a threatening presence with his tall stature and shoulder-length hair. He's probably my age, which doesn't bode well for me, especially if he knows Tessa by name.

"Hey, Darren," she beams.

"What can I get started for you guys?"

"A hot chocolate for him," Tessa turns to wink at me. She knows how much I love hot chocolate. "And I'll get a Grande caramel macchiato, half whole, and have soy milk, foam on top, cinnamon powder, and vanilla syrup."

My eyes widen. That was quite the coffee order.

I take out some cash to pay for both of us until Tessa grabs my hand. "Oh, you don't have to do that," she says reassuringly with a slight tremble in her voice.

"I wasn't going to let you pay for yourself. I don't mind, really," I grin at her while I hand the cash to the cashier.

"Well, thank you." She blushes. Thank you, Google, for another brilliant suggestion.

We move to the other side of the coffee bar to wait for our drinks. "I take it you come here a lot."

"Hey, when you're a loner, and the only place you find some peace is in a coffee shop, you figure out what you like," Tessa replies.

I feel a pang of empathy. I don't have a lot of friends. Never have. However, the way Tessa said that her not having friends is beyond her control, and it bothers her. I can relate to her in the solitary side of life, but I never minded it.

We take our drinks and go back to our table. "I don't really have friends either," I empathize with her. "Except my dad. And Mason. And my computer."

Tessa suddenly starts to giggle but tries to hide it. I do a quick run-through in my brain of everything I've said that could have been humorous, but I come up empty.

"What's so funny?" I lightly chuckle.

"Nothing," she says while muffling her giggles with her hand. "It's just when you said your computer was your friend, my mind went straight to the gutter."

My brows pinch together, trying to understand her thinking. Why would she – Oh. Crap.

She thinks I use it to watch...*ahem*...videos.

That's what she thought I meant. I need to nip that in the bud because she's still laughing. As glad as I am that she's enjoying herself, I do *not* want her to think I'm some horny teenager.

"That didn't come out right." I wave my hands around, trying to rectify the mess I created. Then I started to laugh with her. "That's not what I meant –"

"It's okay, I know," she pats my arm while recovering from her giggle fest. "I thought it was funny."

Relief washes over me, and I feel my face cool down from turning completely red. I begin to laugh harder, and Tessa joins right back in without missing a beat.

Just from that, I know we'll get along just fine.

"So, how was school this week?" I inquire, sipping my drink. Need to start with something we have in common: our lack of concern for doing anything related to school.

With a sly grin, Tessa answers, "I have skipped a lot, this week. My parents have no idea since they're constantly working."

Tessa has never revealed anything about her home life since we met. I have a feeling there's something deeper about her relationship with her parents, but I don't know if I should pry yet, so I decided to play it cool. "You're lucky. If I skipped, it would never escape my dad. He would get a phone call immediately. I mean, my Algebra teacher called him a couple of weeks ago to tell him I was failing, and I got lectured about it."

"At least your dad cares," she points out, then mumbles, "My parents have no clue that I'm probably not going to graduate this year. They don't care, and neither do I." Tessa sips from her cup, finishing her statement.

With the tone she used – saddened, lonely, and angry – I can tell it bothers her that her parents aren't present in her life. She lashes out by being a rebellious student. I guess that's what I'm doing also: lashing out by being a rebellious student.

"I probably won't graduate either," I tell her, trying to make her feel less alone.

"Look at us. Looking at success right in the eyes." She lifts her cup in a "cheers" motion. "Have you written anything new?"

It appears we're keeping this surface level. I can handle that.

"Trying to write up another segment of the snowfield story, but I'm stuck. So, I've been jotting down ideas for other short stories."

"Did my ideas not help you?" she questions with a frown.

Oh, shoot. I didn't mean to make her feel bad. *Fix this now!* "It's not that at all. Your ideas were good. I'm just having a hard time figuring out where to go from those ideas."

"Oh, okay," she nods, satisfied with my answer.

Thank god. "What about you? Have you drawn anything new?" I quickly move on to something else.

"I actually finished the first page of the comic I wanted to write, so progress, thanks to you," Tessa weakly raises her fist in the air. I don't know if she could be any cuter. "Your questions gave me some ideas to bring the story together."

"That's good, keep it up. You'll feel better each time you finish a project like that."

"I do." Her eyes turn contemplative when she turns to the window. "You know, sometimes I wish I had friends to share this kind of stuff with."

I lean in, eyes narrowed at her. "So you have no friends? At all?"

"See, that's the other reason I skip school," she says while wiggling her finger at me, smirking to hide the sting she no doubt feels regularly. "I usually get made fun of because I like spending my time drawing in the library. Girls call me a loner—a weirdo. Then, when they find out I don't have a boyfriend, I get teased for being a virgin. It's easier to avoid it all. My parents won't understand, so I don't tell them. It's not like they're around enough to do anything about it."

Girls are awful, making fun of someone because they like to draw. Or because they're a virgin. Or because they prefer to be alone. Nothing is wrong with any of this, yet she's being bullied for it.

"I get it." I twist the sleeve on my cup just to do something with my hands. "I'm sorry you have to go through that."

She shrugs like it's no big deal, masking her feelings. "It's okay. At least I have you." A wave of insecurity coats her expression. "It's okay that I consider you my friend, right?"

It pains me that she feels so afraid. Afraid of losing friendships. Afraid of gaining friendships. Afraid of having something more than friendship. Which, to be frank, is what I hoped we would be after this date, even though she called me a friend. Maybe she needs a friend more than a romantic relationship. I can give her that, at the very least.

"Of course," I say as genuinely as I can. "I'm a loyal person. If you want me in your life, I'll stay as long as you have me."

Her lips tug slightly into a smile. "I knew I would like you," she says with a wink and takes a sip from her cup.

I sip from my cup as well to hide my reddened cheeks. It seems like Tessa is flirting with me, and I'm not used to girls flirting with me. I don't know how to handle it or what to say.

My once racing heart that was present at the beginning of this date has slowed to a normal rhythm. Conversation is easy; we've been able to laugh, and we found some things in common. Something I've never found in a conversation with a girl. It's refreshing.

"I swear, he thought it looked like a happy sperm!" Tessa finishes a story as she sips her coffee. "Seeing the horror on his face made my day."

I throw my head back and laugh. When she told me about the first thing she ever drew, I didn't expect the story to include balloons that looked like sperm that she showed to her teacher. Which is fine because it's cool to know a girl isn't too shy to mention stuff like that. In fact, it's kind of hot.

We've been talking for the last hour or so. Nothing too deep, just talking about her art and *Family Guy*. Which is fine, it leaves me something to anticipate later. I've nursed my hot chocolate the entire time, which has gone cold now. When you're so engaged in conversation, you forget about your drink; that must mean it's a good date. Your surroundings even fade into the background, and it's just you and the person you're with.

Tessa peeks at her watch and gasps. "Wow, it's already five! How have we not been kicked out already?"

I take a quick glance around the coffee shop. It's getting dark outside, and most people have cleared out. The only sounds present are the whirrs of espresso machines and blenders.

"We should probably leave before they close," I say. I get up, and my legs are completely stiff, another good sign that I've thoroughly enjoyed this time with her. I gather our empty cups and head to the trash.

"Oh, thank you," she says, surprised.

Once I come back, I extend my elbow for Tessa to take. "I'll walk you to your car."

"It's like fifty feet away. Are we going to a ball?" she teases.

"I'm trying to be a gentleman," I say with a shrug.

Tessa brushes stray hairs from her eyes and stuffs it under her beanie. "Okay, okay, I'll let you be a gentleman," she relents, looping her arm with mine.

We reach her car, a brand new 2006 Honda Civic. It makes sense; if her parents are constantly working, that means she has money, which means she has the best of everything. I'm beginning to wonder what she sees in me, practically a peasant.

She lets go of my arm. "Thank you for getting together with me. I don't remember the last time I laughed that hard."

"I don't either."

Her cheeks have the cutest shade of red. This must be new for her, too.

"Thank you for agreeing to go out with me," I add.

"Well, I had nothing better to do," she says coolly.

She must see my face fall because Tessa covers her mouth with her hand in complete shame. "Oh my god, that didn't come out the way I wanted. I'm so sorry! I was trying to say it was a good way to spend the day."

"I didn't think you were being mean, Tessa," I say. "You're too sweet to be mean."

"I'm glad you think so," she nods, cheeks reddening as she studies the ground and combs a strand of hair behind her ear.

We stand there in silence for a second, and then an unfamiliar emotion hits me: yearning. I don't want this date to end. I want to spend more time with her. It's hard for me to find people I'm comfortable with, and not once have I felt this comfortable with a girl.

She's still standing there, not saying anything, not moving to open her car door. I'm not sure what the protocol is here. I was so engrossed in what to do during a date that I failed to prepare for the "after date" expectations. From the movies I've seen, some girls expect a first kiss, while some don't want to appear too eager, so the first kiss is put on hold. A hug is a recipe to make things super awkward. A handshake is even worse than a hug. So, with that conundrum, my hands stay inside the pockets of my baggy jeans.

I clear my throat and back away to head to my car. "Have a good night, Tessa."

With each step I take, all I feel is a nagging voice telling me to find an excuse to keep this date going. The last thing I want is to go home with a reminder of what I have to face every day. Throughout our lives, when it comes to making decisions, people – teachers, parents, peers – tell us to go with what our heart says. Right now, my heart is telling me this date isn't over yet.

Follow your heart.

I turn on my heel and walk back to her car in wide strides, where she just closed her passenger side door. "I just realized something."

Tessa turns back to me with a hint of hope. "Yes?"

"I'm not ready to go home yet."

She breathes out in relief. "Thank god. I'm not either."

"Well, what do you want to do?"

"Go somewhere where there are no people," she says with a giggle.

I think about it for a moment. I don't know Federal Way very well, so I'm not sure what's around for us to do. We are close to Puget Sound, though. From movies I've seen growing up, girls like hanging out by the water with their love interests, sitting on a car roof, watching the sunset, making out, all of that.

The place I have in mind doesn't have an environment conducive to sitting on a car roof or going to the beach, but it's the perfect scenic view.

"This is incredible!" Tessa says as we make our way to the entrance of the Bowl, Stadium High School's football field. Right at the gate is an impeccable view of Commencement Bay. Mr. Nichol has an even better view in his office, but this view works.

Tessa grips the iron bars of the gate to get a clearer view. She's entirely mesmerized by the picturesque scenery, while I'm mesmerized by her beautiful face. I can't help but take in the softness of her skin, her plump lips, her chocolate brown eyes that brighten when she talks about something she's passionate about, and the beanie that covers her head but leaves her brownish-red hair to frame her face.

"Yeah, it's cool, I guess," I say with indifference.

"You guess?" she drops her jaw and smacks me on the arm. "It's beautiful out here. My school looks like a freaking prison!"

I take in the scenery, trying to see it from her point of view. I've been coming to this school for three years now, so I've gotten used to the location and the view. But I can't say I've ever seen the water from here when it's dark outside. City lights sparkle and reflect off the water's surface in hues of orange and red and expand up to the shore on the other side. It gives a romantic feel to it.

Wow. Now it's like I'm seeing it for the first time.

"You're a lucky guy, Seth," Tessa's soft voice breaks my trance.

Her words ruminate in my head as we stare out into the water. I should feel lucky. Sometimes, I don't, but in this moment, right now, I finally do. Instead of being at home on a Saturday night as I usually am, I'm on a date with a girl who wants to spend time with me.

When everything with Mom went down, it became easy to focus on what I didn't have. Motivation. Drive. Goals. Parents that love and respect each other. What I fail to realize is that what I have outweighs those things. I have a dad that cares about me despite what he's going through. I have Mason to make life interesting, and he has my back (sometimes).

Now, I have Tessa. If she'll have me.

"I am lucky," I lead in. I pause because not once have I laid my heart on the table like I'm about to do now. Never in my life have I admitted to having feelings for a girl to her face. "I feel lucky that I met you."

"You do?" she stutters, blushing hard as if no one has said anything like that to her before.

I've already laid out my hand; I might as well lay out the rest of the deck. "I don't know about you, but meeting you has been the best thing that's ever happened to me," I admit, gripping the iron bars of the gate and swallowing hard. "You give me something to look forward to. Like my life is starting to have some sort of purpose; it's been a long time since I've felt that way, Tessa."

Tessa is frozen in place, not saying anything. Panic sets in when I realize I may have said too much too soon.

Attempting to break awkward tension, I add, "and I'm grateful for this view, too." I throw in an awkward laugh, but Tessa is silent. Her eyes well up with tears, sparkling in the evening light. Anxiety rips through me, worried that I've ruined this date.

That is until I see the corner of her mouth tug upward. She's happy. Those are happy tears. Relief replaces the tension I was feeling seconds ago.

She puts a hand on her chest and swallows. "I don't have any friends, Seth," she speaks quietly. "Unless you count the ones I've met on Gaia. Yet somehow, by chance, you plop right into my life." She quickly wipes her eyes with the sleeve of her sweatshirt. "You're the friend in my life I didn't know I needed."

My brows furrow as I study her. She's mentioned friends three times now. To her, I'm only a friend. This outing wasn't a date but friends getting together for coffee. After tonight, I thought she would want to be more than just friends. *I* want to be more than that. If friendship is all she can offer, then I will learn to live with that. I'd rather have that than nothing at all with her. She's become too important for me to lose.

I can't go home tonight without straightening that out.

"So, you want to be…just friends?" I ask and hold my breath for the answer.

"Um, well, I…" Her throat bobs as she swallows, gazing away from me as she ponders her next words. I mentally prepare myself for the letdown.

"Okay, I'm just going to say it," she exhales sharply. "I've wanted to kiss you since we left Starbucks, but I didn't want to freak you out. Being here, with you, getting to know you, and sharing the same struggles makes it almost impossible for me to avoid it."

My heart freezes at her admission, veins racing with anticipation and nervous excitement. My palms start to sweat. I've never been kissed, and I have a cute, innocent, beautiful girl who just admitted that she wants to kiss me. The fact that my first date will possibly end in my first kiss makes me weak in the knees.

Before I realize what I'm doing, my hand extends, and my finger strokes her cheek. Something I've wanted to do since I saw her. "Maybe I don't want you to avoid it."

As if that was all the permission she needed, she snaked her arm around my neck and pulled me in for a kiss. At first, it's a feather-light touch of our lips, but I feel the electricity of it down to my toes. We pull away for a moment, already missing her soft lips, our eyes making a silent agreement to do that again. I take her face in my hands and kiss her deeper. My mind is a multi-track center with a plethora of feelings and thoughts crashing into each other as our mouths move in sync with each other, her lips addictively soft and warm against mine. Among the variety of thoughts traveling across my mind, I wonder how I went this long without experiencing something that feels so good. So, so good.

Sparks. Fireworks. Blinking lights. I feel them all explode between us. Everything – the city lights, the scenery, the school, the night sky – fades into the background.

We pull apart, and I lean my forehead onto hers, breathing heavily from the intensity of it all.

"And I'm lucky you were my first kiss," I whisper.

Tessa pulls me into an embrace. "Same here," she mumbles into my chest.

I don't hesitate to hold her in return. This, right here, feels right. This is what I've been looking for. What I've been waiting for. Yet, as I hold her, all I wonder is how my mom could have ever ditched my dad if, at one point, they felt this way about each other. I don't understand how anyone could throw away something like this. People that make you feel the way Tessa is making me feel right now don't come around very often.

"Seth?"

"Yeah?"

"Are we a couple now?"

My face breaks out into a wide grin. That's exactly what I've been wondering since we left Starbucks. I also keep wondering if I'm truly ready for that. Before we met face-to-face, I wasn't sure if I wanted to make that leap right away. Now that I've met her, the desire to move forward is becoming more and more real.

There's one thing I vow to myself, and that I will vow to her. No matter what changes come up in our lives, I will be there for her every step of the way. I refuse to give up on her.

I break our embrace and take her face in my hands. "I will be loyal. I will see this through, no matter what happens." I kiss her on the forehead to seal the deal. "I'll stick with you as long as you'll have me. I promise."

Tessa kisses the corner of my mouth, sending tingles from head to toe. "Thank you."

CHAPTER 4

During the last remaining moments of English class, I go through my story idea in my journal. This time, I want to do a short story about a group of teens finding an abandoned train track. Living close to the Tacoma waterfront, it's normal to see train tracks all over the place, with very old boxcars and containers placed on them. It got me thinking of a story idea that goes with the kind of genre I write about. As usual, I wrote it all out during class and didn't pay any attention to what Mrs. Buhler was saying.

Eventually, my eyes strayed to the seat next to me, where the dark blonde girl sat next to me. She had earbuds on, her hair was tied into a mid-ponytail, and her eyes squinted in concentration on a stack of paper in front of her. She flips the page over, and I briefly catch a glimpse of the word "chapter" on it.

Does she write too?

Although Tessa has been good with giving me a variety of ideas, she's not as much a writer as she is an artist. I still love collaborating with her and seeing her talents come to life on a canvas or in digital form. It's just nice to meet other writers as well. It also doesn't hurt that this girl is cute and has a pretty face. Although, she shows a hint of sorrow with the frown on her lips. Her presence emanates one of sweetness, yet I want to know why she looks so down.

The bell rings, and everyone packs their stuff. I grab my backpack and stand up, waiting for everyone else to exit the classroom. The girl shoots up from her seat, her book clutched tightly to her chest with her binder, and swings her backpack on in a swift motion, blending with the students also trying to exit the classroom. Obviously, something is bothering her, or she's having a bad day. Unfortunately for her, I watch as it gets worse very fast.

She trips.

Her binder falls to the floor.

Pages fly all over the hallway.

"Are you freaking kidding me?" she whispers to herself. I find myself cringing on her behalf. There's nothing more embarrassing than being in a complete mess. According to the tears brimming in her eyes, she's embarrassed and has reached her limit for the day. On top of that, kids are classic morons and step around her and her story that has scattered all over the hallway. Even Mason hops over her.

"Sorry, Ree-Ree, I'm in a hurry; okay, bye," he takes off, running down the hall.

"Man whore," she mutters under her breath as she picks up her mess, earbuds dangling in front of her. Of course, he's rushing to spend time with Harmony before she goes to her next class. If she doesn't get the hint now that he likes her, all hope is lost.

Losing faith in all humanity and my best friend, I bend down on my knees and pick up the papers. The girl sniffles when she lifts her head and sees me.

"Thank you," she says through bouts of sniffles.

"No problem."

When we stand back up, I finally get a full view of the girl that sits in front of Mason, the girl who laughed at his "shriveling privates" statement. Light makeup on her face, short stature, lips turned up in a sweet and embarrassed smile, and a fruity and sweet scent that intoxicates my senses. Her hair and bangs frame her face and fall around a pair of big, green eyes full of unshed tears.

To prevent myself from checking her out more, I find that I still have one of the pages of her story in my hand. I flip it over to look at what looks like a title page. "Legend of the Knight? A Knight's Duel?"

She snatches the paper from my hands, her timid nature making an appearance. She organizes the pages in her hand to distract herself, paying a lot of attention to the floor. Fortunately, I have the perfect icebreaker for her uneasiness.

"You like to write?"

"Yeah," she answers with a nod, her stance telling me she's waiting for me to tease her.

"I do, too," I reply.

That makes her take out her headphones and finally meet my eyes. "Really?"

"Yeah," I confirm with all the sincerity I have. With a shrug, I add, "I mean, short stories. I've never been able to write a book. What kind of stories do you write?"

"I've been in a medieval phase lately, as you saw with the titles I'm working with. I can't do short stories to save my life, as you can see." She gestures to the papers in her arms.

"Every writer has the thing that works for them," I reassure her. "Hey, maybe I can read your story sometime. I'm always looking for writers to collaborate with. Exchange ideas, stuff like that. If you want."

Just like that, the switch I ignited in her turns off when she frowns. Something about the idea of sharing her writing scares her. Maybe she only writes for herself, not to be a published writer. Only lets certain people read her work.

"I'm editing it right now," she says warily, shifting her weight.

"Maybe when it's ready then," I suggest.

She scoffs. "By the time it's ready, you'll forget all about it," she says sheepishly.

"No, I'll remember. I'll make sure to ask you about it every day from now on."

"Oh, how I look forward to that," she says with humor.

"I know you're being sarcastic, but I'm true to my word."

"I'll believe it when I see it." Then she leans in and loudly whispers, "Besides, I don't know your name."

"Oh, duh," I roll my eyes and slap myself on the forehead. I hold out my hand. "I'm Seth. Seth Harris."

She stifles a smile and blushes when she shakes my hand. "Seth Harris," she repeats. "I'm Marie. Marie Burn."

"I see you're teasing me. Nice," I point out.

"Sorry, I had to," Marie giggles and pats my shoulder.

"Marie *Burn*, huh?" I feign shock. "Sounds kind of violent."

"Well, my ancestors would be proud if they knew that my parents took advantage of that with my middle name," she quips with a close-lipped smile.

Now, this conversation just got a lot more fun. Intrigued, I adjust my beat-up backpack and lean closer to her. "What's your middle name?"

Marie exhales sharply and has regret written all over her. "Katharine," she confesses gently and waits in anticipation for me to figure it out and make fun of her. All she can see on my face is confusion, though.

Marie Katharine Burn. I say it silently to myself. It sounds so familiar, but I can't pinpoint the reason why. Where have I heard that name?

"Katharine Burn," Marie assists me.

My eyes brighten in recognition. "Like Katharine Hepburn?"

"Exactly. And now I regret sharing that tidbit with a stranger," she sighs, then waves in invitation. "Okay, come on. Bring on the jokes."

"No jokes here. Your secret is safe with me," I salute, then say with a shrug, "If it helps, my middle name is Kyle. There. Now, we're not strangers."

That gets a giggle out of her. "Not really a tease-worthy name, but thank you for trying to make me feel better."

"Worth a shot."

She smiles back, twirling her body back and forth, waiting for one of us to end the conversation. I don't make a move to leave either, though, mainly because I don't have a good exit strategy for these kinds of situations.

The one-minute bell goes off. Too bad that this is the one time I want to skip class altogether and keep talking to her. Pull a Tessa and go somewhere.

She points her thumb over her shoulder. "I should go." Then she bows at me as if I'm some kind of royalty, which gets one of those genuine laughs out of me. "Nice to meet you, Seth Kyle Harris."

"You too, Marie Katharine Hepburn," I joke, then clears my throat. "Excuse me, Burn."

She rolls her eyes and makes her way down the hallway. I wave goodbye and stroll down the hallway, wondering what in the world just happened.

There's a new seating arrangement in Microsoft Academy when I show up. I always hated it when teachers changed the seating since it meant I'd have to sit next to another stranger I didn't care to associate myself with. Dang it.

As I get settled in my new seat and grumble inwardly about who will end up sitting with me, I find Marie entering the classroom. I feel a smile creep on my face when I watch her find her new seat. I had no idea she had this class. I feel much better about my situation.

She makes her way over to me and takes the empty seat next to me. "Oh hey, Katharine Burn," I greet her as she plops her backpack on the floor.

"Hey, it's Seth Kyle Harris," she says cheerfully as if the fiasco from this morning is long forgotten. "I still don't have any creative names for you. I hope sitting with you will get the ball rolling. I can stare at you like a Peeping Tom till something comes to mind."

"As long as you occasionally tell me I'm pretty, do what you need to," I smirk.

Mr. Niendorf tells us to work from a page in our textbooks that requires using Microsoft Word. This will be easy; I use Word every single day. I can type like nobody's business.

Maybe I'll actually do the assignment. Then, I can spend the rest of the time emailing Tessa. I can't wait to see her, live our introverted ways, and relive our first kiss. Man, that was a great night.

I open Microsoft Word and stare at the blank document in front of me. This is going to be more work than I expected. Now, I don't want to do it at all. All of my motivation has been zapped, and all I want to do is check my email.

Screw this. I'm checking my email.

Tessa and I decided to send photos of each other to look at on days we don't see each other, something to make us smile when we miss each other. She sent me a picture of herself holding up two fingers, brown eyes sparkling, and wearing a grin underneath a black beanie with a picture of a cat's face on it. What has me smiling is her caption.

I don't have anything with Black Panther on it, so my cat beanie will have to do.

Just recently, I found out Black Panther is her other favorite Marvel hero. Just based on his bulletproof costume and retractable claws, he's my favorite, too.

Dear Tessa,

You look beautiful as always. I'll send you a photo when I get home. Next time we hang out, we should take a photo together. – Seth

Once I send the email, I lean back in my chair and sigh. This girl is a keeper. And she's all mine.

I hear the sound of paper sliding in my direction, and I turn to see Marie's hand retreat from a folded paper, and she's back to looking at her screen like nothing happened. I open the paper and read her note.

YOU LOOK BORED.

It's just three words, yet it makes me chuckle. I don't remember the last time I engaged in passing notes, but I'm pretty sure it involved talking to Mason about figuring out how to ask a girl to a dance. Needless to say, it never happened.

`What was your first clue?`

I slide the paper back to her with my response, and I hear her hold in laughter from the puffs from her nose. She picks up her pencil and writes back.

This continues for a while.

WELL, FOR ONE THING, YOU'RE NOT DOING THE ASSIGNMENT.

`You're not either if you're writing notes to me.`

I'VE ALREADY FINISHED IT, AND THE NEXT LESSON ISN'T TILL TOMORROW, SO I'M IN THE CLEAR.

`Overachiever. Was it really obvious I was bored?`

YES. YOU NEED TO IMPROVE YOUR STEALTH. NOW, THE REAL REASON I STARTED THIS CONVERSATION IS I WANTED TO KNOW IF YOU WANNA PLAY A GAME.

This is interesting. Marie appears to be slacking off as well. I'm all for it, especially if it means I can get away with not doing this dreaded assignment.

`Sure. What are we playing?`

I CAN START BY ASKING YOU A QUESTION, AND AFTER YOU ANSWER, YOU HAVE TO ASK THE SAME QUESTION IN RETURN, THEN, IT'S YOUR TURN TO ASK SOMETHING ELSE. MAKE SENSE?

`Sounds good. You go first =)`

OK, HMMM...ARE YOU A CAT OR DOG PERSON?

Out of all the questions she could ask someone she just met, I didn't see this one coming. I guess she's no ordinary girl. She's not afraid to be herself and doesn't mind being teased.

I pass the note back to her, keeping my expression completely stoic. The less Mr. Niendorf suspects I'm doing nothing, the better.

Here I was, expecting a question like "Where are you from?" and you asked me about animals. You continue to surprise me.

Okay. Where are you from?

Haha, nice try. I'm a dog person through and through. You?

Worried it would be a boring start. Gotta keep you interested somehow. Otherwise, you'd probably rather do the assignment than talk to me ☺ Cats, all the way. I'm going to be a CCL when I grow old.

This is the best alternative to doing any assignment. By the way, CCL?

Crazy Cat Lady. Cats are the best. There's a reason men are called dogs ;)

The wit of this girl is unlike anything I've ever seen. It's enough to make an introvert like me uncomfortable. Yet I find myself intrigued to see what happens if I keep this conversation going.

There's a plethora of questions I could ask. Favorite food is a boring one. I need to narrow it down since we're doing "this or that" type of questions.

Thank you for telling me how you feel about men. May I suggest you stay as far away from the male race as possible :) Hmmm, let's see. Burritos or tacos?

I knew I liked you, lol. Burritos, every time. You?

I love burritos myself. Your turn.

Yay, we're burrito twins!

I can't help but quietly laugh when I write back.

First, you say you're going to hoard cats when you grow old, now you're calling us burrito twins, and

I'm going along with it. I'm starting to question our
sanity.

Is that a bad thing?

Weird is never a bad thing. The good kind of weird,
anyway.

There's such a thing as good weird?

Yes. I'm a good weird, in case you were wondering.
Consider yourself warned.

Warning received. Does this mean we're friends?

I take a moment to reflect on this. I don't have a lot of friends, but with the kind of personality Marie has, though, it wouldn't be so irritating or burdensome to have her as a friend. If anything, I can see her being a bright light at the end of the dark tunnel that is my life.

We became friends this morning, so yes, we are. And
it's still your turn.

We continue this game for a while. I learned that she grew up in Tacoma on the other side of the bay, her parents have been divorced for a few months, she lives with her mom, and has expressed her undying love for Snickers. It is weirdly convenient that her parents divorced around the same time mine did.

Before I know it, the bell rings, and school is over. I was so engrossed in this note exchange that I didn't care what time it was or the fact that this was the last class of the day. At least I can finally say school ended on a fun note, literally and figuratively.

In the parking garage, I end up walking behind Marie towards my own car. That is until she stops at a baby blue Mazda Miata convertible. As she swings her backpack off her back and tosses it in the backseat, I'm taken back to the first time I ever rode a convertible.

My parents and I took a trip to L.A. when I was about thirteen years old. My mom's dream was to ride along the Pacific Coast Highway in a convertible, as shown in the movies. To surprise her, my dad rented one for the day since renting it for the whole trip would have cost as much as a house payment. My mom wasted no time in taking the bright red Mustang and driving full speed toward the highway, enjoying the ocean views among the winding roads. I loved seeing Mom so happy, and it was a memory I always held dear. Now, it's just painful.

Out of sheer curiosity, I stopped to admire her car. "That your car?"

Marie jumps and faces me, caught off guard. "Oh. Yeah," she replies, clearing her throat. "It's the one thing we were able to keep after my parents split. Mom lets me take it on nice days like this."

"That's so cool." I round the car, taking in its beauty. I smooth my hand over the trunk. "I rode in a convertible once. My parents and I drove along the Pacific Coast Highway, and oh man, it was such a blast." I turn reminiscent and sigh. "I actually kind of miss it."

"Aw, that sounds so fun," she says with positivity. "Maybe I can take you for a spin sometime," she suggests with a shy shrug. "Maybe I'll even let you drive it as long as you can confirm that you're a safe driver. My mom would stop my heart if anything happened to this thing."

"Yeah, that would be cool!" I exclaim a little too loudly. I clear my throat and right myself. "Uh, yeah, that would be fun. I'm a safe driver and all." My eyes roam over the sleek exterior and light beige leather seats. "You're lucky you have one of these."

"I know. Yay, divorce!" Marie raises her arm like a cheerleader and laughs, and then cringes at herself. I laugh at her awkwardness, taking one last glance at the car. It would be incredible to relive that memory of riding the coast, wind blowing through our hair, music blasting in the air.

Shaking my head, I back away and wave at her. "Have a good day, Marie."

"Thanks, you too," she waves back at me, hopping over the door and landing in the driver's seat instead of actually opening the door.

As she drives away, she blasts "Best of Both Worlds" by Van Halen through her stereo, rocking out with her head bobbing and bouncing side to side in her seat, zero shame in who's watching her, including me. I haven't heard that song since I was a kid, and my dad would play his Van Halen *5150* album on the CD player in his car. I stand there in the middle of the garage, listening until the music fades in the distance.

To say this has been an interesting day is an understatement. I met a very quirky, funny, shining girl that I found myself, a true introvert, talking to most of the day.

Changes in my life are happening in the most unexpected ways, and I can't say I mind it.

CHAPTER 5

"Wow, there's hardly anybody here," Tessa notices, drinking from her coffee cup with gloved hands. This time, she got a large soymilk latte with a pump of French vanilla syrup, mocha sauce, and cinnamon powder steamed into the milk. I don't know how she memorizes all these complicated drinks that she orders. All I need is cocoa to make me happy.

Apparently, Tessa's favorite pastime is people-watching—specifically, people-watching by herself. I can't say I've ever done this before, but here we are, in November, at Steel Lake Park, sitting far away from the public eye under a tree. Tessa prepared for the cold, more than I did, with her puffy jacket, gloves, and Ugg boots. The only winter gear I managed to find was a pair of combat boots and a black hoodie, and of course, the only gloves I cared to wear were my infamous fingerless ones. It worked in my favor when Tessa kissed me and said I looked "sexy."

"Why are we so far away from everyone?" I wonder. "Can you even see what people are doing?"

"I may like watching people, but it doesn't mean I want them watching me," she answers.

"At this point, all you're missing is a pair of binoculars," I tease with a nudge to her arm.

"No, that's where I draw the line," Tessa retorts.

I sip from my hot cocoa, letting the heat warm me up. "Do you normally do this in the fall?"

"Sometimes. I'm not a fan of the cold, so I end up staying locked up in my room watching reality shows," Tessa shrugs. "That's my indoor version of people-watching."

"And eating popcorn?" I add.

Tessa giggles and cuddles up next to me, burrowing her head in the crook of my arm. "And eating popcorn."

We sit in silence for a few moments, staring out at families playing with their kids at the playground or people hanging out at the dock. She may be enamored with this activity, but all I can think about is how much I enjoy having her so close to me, her black beanie grazing the stubble of my chin when I take in her cuteness. We're at the point in this relationship where it's extremely difficult not being together. I don't know about her, but I feel suffocated when I'm not around her. I need to be with her more.

"So, I was thinking," I begin, "What if we go to the pumpkin patch tomorrow? Seems like something couples do together in the fall."

"Hmm," Tessa straightens up, uncertainty painted on her face. "There's going to be so many people there since it's fall and everything."

"Let's go after school, then," I suggest. "It'll be early afternoon, and there won't be a lot of people around."

"That's true," she replies with a mischievous lilt. With a grin, she shifts her weight to face me. "What if we just skipped tomorrow?"

My brows scrunch together. "What?"

"Yeah. Why don't we just leave school in the middle of the day and go to the pumpkin patch? There will hardly be anybody there, and we would have at least made an appearance."

I hate going to school, but I never thought about skipping altogether. Stadium is very strict when it comes to students skipping, especially when you try to leave in the middle of the day without a note. How will I be able to skip and keep it from my dad? Can I even pull it off?

"I don't know," I say with reluctance. "I think my dad will eventually find out. And I'm not a good liar."

"Oh, come on." Tessa groans and shakes my arm. "We already know we're not graduating, so why torture ourselves by going?"

She has a point there. Maybe I can play off that I'm sick and sneak out. I'll trying anything so I don't have to go to the one place that reminds me of my mom's values.

"Okay, I guess I'll try it," I cave in.

Tessa claps happily and wraps her arms around my torso. "This is going to be fun!" she shrieks.

I agree. I just hope it's worth it.

All of a sudden, I hear the *click* of a camera that makes me jump in surprise. "What –" I start to say when Tessa busts out laughing.

"Didn't mean to scare you. Just wanted pictures of you for when I don't see you." She rolls the rewind on the camera for the next picture.

I wrap my arm around her, holding her close to me. "Let's take one together then."

"Our first picture as a couple!" she giggles and angles the camera in front of us. I smile genuinely, knowing that when we look back on these photos, we'll remember it as the start of the best thing that could ever happen to us.

"Admit it, you got a thrill from skipping today," Tessa elbows me as we meander along the many lanes of pumpkins.

Originally, I didn't know how I was going to pull this off without being caught. Tessa drove to my school in the drop-off area, and I played it off like I was going to the auxiliary building across the courtyard but went down the steps and hopped in her car.

"It's definitely something I can cross off my bucket list," I reply, trudging through the dirt in my combat boots, checking out the different-sized pumpkins. There's only a couple of people around, just the way Tessa wanted it. I don't care to be around a lot of people either, but she has a strong aversion to it for some reason.

I bend down to look at a small pumpkin. "I remember doing this as a kid," I reminisce. "Going with mom to the pumpkin patch. She'd challenge me to pick the biggest one and try to lift it. If I could pick up, that was the one we got to take home. Of course, I'd topple over and fall on my butt, and then Mom would have to carry it for me." I chuckle to myself at the memory and stand back up. "What about you? Did you have any traditions in your family?"

Tessa scoffs. "Yeah, when they didn't live for their jobs." Her gaze shifts to the ground as she softly kicks at the dirt. "You should pick up a heavy pumpkin and take one home," she tells me after she clears her throat.

That's the way this relationship has been. I tell her more about my history than she tells me about hers. I want to know what makes Tessa who she is, but she refuses to go down that path. Over time, I've learned to accept that.

"No. I don't want to make it obvious to my dad where I've been."

"Do it for me," Tessa says flirtatiously. "Put those arm muscles to work!"

Rolling my eyes, I search the expanse of land for the biggest pumpkin I can find. They all look so gigantic; they could all qualify to turn into Cinderella's carriage. Especially the one I'm eyeing right now. It has to be at least fifty pounds.

I bend down to pick it up and use my legs to lift it up, and holy crap is it heavy.

"Yay, you did it!" Tessa shouts and whips out her camera to take a picture. Once she's done, I plop the pumpkin down on the ground with a thud.

"Oh no, I think you broke it," Tessa says worriedly, bending down to check it.

"Oh crap, really?" I go next to Tessa to see what she's looking at, but when I hear her break down in laughter and I see no sign of a broken pumpkin, I know she had me fooled.

"You suck," I gently shove her shoulder as she keeps laughing.

"So, out again with Tessa today, huh?" Dad grumbles when I come into the kitchen.

I should probably mention that Dad isn't supportive of my relationship with Tessa. She helped me skip school a couple more times. On one of the days, we went to the waterfront, took photos, and kissed under the sunset. Another time, we just hung out at her house and watched movies. Her parents are gone all the time anyway, so we get away with it. At first, I felt iffy about it, but I decided to just enjoy the moment. It's been incredible, and I find myself falling harder for her every day.

"Yup," I reply in a clipped manner.

"You've been seein' a lot of her lately," Dad mentions skeptically. He grabs a beer from the fridge and sits at the kitchen table. He moves in a way that he's pondering his next words. He knows something but doesn't know how to say it.

I shrug. "Well, yeah, she's my girlfriend."

Dad takes a sip of his beer pensively. "Is she worth it?"

My brows pinch together, confused about where he's getting at. "Is what worth it?"

Dad folds his arms and narrows his eyes at me. "Your failin' grades. Skippin' school. You know, all that rebellious stuff."

My whole body freezes. I try to play off my lie again, but it's very unconvincing. "I was sick –"

"Save it," he snaps, his demeanor switching from inquisitive to angry. "I'm not stupid! You think the school doesn't call me when you miss your classes?"

Worth a shot. Deep down, I knew I wouldn't be able to get away with this for too long.

"You need to cut this girl off," he demands adamantly. "She's not good for you."

"You're the one that said I need to find something that motivates me," I point at him. "Well, she motivates me!"

"To do what?" he shouts.

"To live life! Take risks!"

"No, Seth." He shoots up from his seat and pokes his finger on my chest. "She *prevents* you from livin' life. She takes you away from what you really need to do, and you know it."

I shake my head. "You don't understand."

"No, *you* don't understand. This girl is doin' you no favors. Blame your mother all you want for the way your life is, but you are in charge of your decisions and the consequences that follow."

My breathing grows heavy, my jaw tightening in anger. "You're right. I am in charge of my own life. And Tessa is a part of it."

Dad's eyes turn downhearted, scowling at me one last time before he turns and treads into the office behind the kitchen. I stand there and ruminate over his words.. He doesn't understand that Tessa gets me. She understands my need to escape, and we're there for each other. He doesn't understand that because my mom didn't do that for him.

I am *not* going to turn into her.

Tessa: *Seth, you know I don't like being around people.*

Seth: *I know you don't, but this is the winter formal, Tessa! We should go as a couple. It could be fun now that you have a boyfriend. You can show me off to those snooty bullies.*

Tessa: *It's just going to give me heavy anxiety. You won't have any fun, and you'll want to find some other girls to dance with.*

I lean back in my chair in my room, staring at her last IM. She just informed me that her winter formal was coming up, and she didn't plan on going, but I wanted us to go together. Plus – and I will deny this to anyone who asks me – I'm a good dancer. My parents taught me from a young age.

My mom used to dance in the kitchen whenever she was cooking, and then she would drag me out of my seat in the kitchen and teach me how to slow dance. "One day, you'll meet a girl who will want to dance with you like this," she told me. Then, my dad would come in and dance with her, showing me their best moves. It was one of many memories of my parents where I knew they were so happy. So in love.

Deep down, I know Tessa wants to go with me. I want to show her my smooth dance moves. The problem is, not only is she an anxious person, but she's deathly afraid of losing me because of it, even though I promised my loyalty to her.

I always try to come up with ideas for things to do together, but she rejects all of them because there's going to be people around. The biggest thing we ever did was the pumpkin patch. Otherwise, it's watching TV at her house or going to Starbucks. Not just any Starbucks, but the one close to her house, where she knows the staff and she's a regular customer. I don't mind since I get to be near her, but I would love to treat her to something nice sometimes.

It would be nice if she did something I wanted to do.

Seth: *I only want to dance with you. You're my girl, and I want to take my girl to a dance. I go along with whatever plans you want every time. Can you please give me this one? Take an anxiety pill if you need to.*

Tessa: *You have a point...but I don't even have a dress.*

Seth: *I don't care. Come in a garbage bag if you want to. I just want to do this with you.*

I'm not willing to give in to her excuses to back out. I'll be a pest and ask every single day if I have to.

Tessa: *You're sweet...*

Tessa: *Okay, we'll go. I'm doing this for you and only you* ☺

Seth: *Thank you! You're the best girlfriend I could have ever asked for!*

Tessa: ☺

I spent most of English class trying to think of a good ending for my *Mysterious Snowfield* story. There are so many different twists I can use, but nothing seems to feel right. Even the ideas Tessa gave me didn't work. It would also help if I had an actual name for the main character. I should start there.

My eyes roam the classroom, brain rolling with ideas, until I spot Marie next to me, finishing her assignment and turning it in. How could I have forgotten about Marie? I wanted to collaborate with her to begin with.

Now excited, I rip out a piece of paper from my journal and write her a note. First, I ask her the question I've been asking since I met her.

`Can I read your story?`

I slide the note quietly to Marie. She looks up and sees my hand retreating from the paper, and her whole face lights up. It hits me then how much I enjoy seeing that happy, peaceful face on a regular basis.

Marie picks up a pencil and writes back.

NICE TRY, BUT NO.

`Dang it. One of these days, you'll change your mind. But I do have a question. How do you pick names for your stories? I need help picking a name for mine.`

KEEP DREAMING, BOY. TO ANSWER YOUR QUESTION, I THINK OF TRAITS THAT I WANT THE CHARACTER TO HAVE, AND I THINK OF NAMES THAT SOUND LIKE SOMEONE WITH THOSE TRAITS. SOME PEOPLE DO IT THE OTHER WAY AROUND, WHERE THEY PICK A NAME AND FIND TRAITS FOR THAT PERSON.

`So, what would you name someone who is a curious traveler who wants to do what's right? I'm picturing a short, blonde-haired white guy.`

Marie snorts at my note. Before I can ask what's so funny, the bell rings. I step over to her desk and wait for her to pack up her stuff. She grins at me as she throws her brown leather backpack over her shoulder.

"A blonde, white guy?" she giggles. "So racist."

"That's not being racist, that's me having a vision," I clarify.

"Whatever you say, buddy."

We exit the classroom. Normally, I would go in the opposite direction, but I want to pick her brain, so I follow her to her next class. "So, what name would you pick?"

"Oh." She flinches in surprise to see me next to her. "Right. I think I would say Jason."

I grimace at that suggestion. I didn't picture a "Jason" to match the physical side of my character.

"Okay, not a fan of that. How about Theo?"

I grimace again and shake after every suggestion she makes after that. "Jesse? Bob? Squirtle?"

That gets me laughing, which gets Marie to laugh along with me. She never fails to say something that ends up being hilarious. "Squirtle? We've reached Pokémon names now?"

"Because you rejected all of my suggestions!" she shouts with humor. Other students pass us in a hurry as our steps slow down. "But here's why I picked Jason," she explains. "If he's a traveler and a hiker, then he's probably strong and fit. And being curious means there's risk involved, but he's strong enough to handle it. And doing what's right involves risking one's own comfort, so he's strong in that way, too. So Jason seems to fit that description well."

My head tilts to the ceiling as I think about her reasoning. I didn't realize she put so much thought into matching the character traits with the right name.

"Wow," I finally say, amazed. "You go deep with this stuff."

That makes Marie smile. "Writing is kind of an escape for me. I tend to go deep with it."

"Like it's a chance to escape reality for a while. Live in someone else's world."

"Yes! Exactly!" she exclaims, practically jumping in excitement. I never thought I'd meet someone who understood what that was like, but Marie feels the exact same way I do about it. "Finally, there's someone who understands!"

Finally indeed. I chuckle to myself, amazed to find someone who views writing the way I do: a lifeline. It's not just *similar,* but *exactly* how I feel.

When I realize it's been a few seconds since one of us said something, I break the ice. "Can I read your story?"

"Ha!" Marie bursts out. "No."

"Oh well," I pretend to be defeated. "I'm glad I found someone I could collaborate with." I pat her on the shoulder when we reach her classroom, and I turn to leave. "Thanks, Marie, that helped me a lot."

"Best of luck to you, sire!" she says with a terrible accent and waves excitedly. I freeze in my tracks and examine her. That's the first time I've heard her use an accent, and it's throwing me off. Her pinks turn a cute shade of pink, and she turns away, which makes me laugh.

"What accent is that?"

Marie cringes. "I have no idea. I'm just weird."

It astounds me how much she's able to be her true, weird, bubbly self with no shame. I guess I could learn a thing or two from her. I can be my weird self as well. I wave back and say in an equally awful accent, "No trouble, madam. I shall retreat to my next learning center!"

Marie doubles over in laughter, and I laugh with her. Hard. I haven't laughed that hard in a long time. Not even with Tessa. At the same time, I'm enjoying hearing Marie's laugh. More than I enjoy someone's laugh. It's like music to my ears.

She waves at me one more time and heads into the classroom. I head to mine, replaying our conversation and laughter in my mind.

Normally, I love eating lunch by myself. It gives everyone else the idea that I want to be alone. Unless it's Mason, he's the only guy I am okay eating lunch with. However, today, Mason decided to attend some geeky club meetings, so I'm alone. I actually look forward to it.

With my lunch tray, I go down the stairs to the bottom level of the cafeteria to my normal sitting area. I automatically turn and scan the area, my eyes landing on

Marie, sitting by herself and eating her lunch. She looks very uncomfortable, which is a funny sight, considering how bubbly and confident she appears when talking to others. Usually, she sits with another girl, but for some reason, that girl is missing today.

Marie's my friend, and she's fun to hang out with. She could use some company. And I could use some fun to perk me up to get me through the rest of the day.

"Oh hey," she greets me cheerfully, her face brightening up immediately, and she sits up straight when I sit in front of her.

"You're by yourself today?"

Her cheeks redden for some reason, followed by a shy grin. "My best friend had an appointment, so she had to leave early. You're not usually by yourself, are you?"

I shake my head and put some fries in my mouth. "Sometimes I eat with Mason. He had some sort of geeky club meeting today. Something involving computers." I wave my hand dismissively. "Whatever it is, it's geeky."

"You're a good friend to remember so clearly what he's doing," Marie teases.

"Listen, I'm a very good friend. I'm sitting with you instead of sitting by myself like I would normally do if Mason wasn't around."

"Are you saying I have a gravitational pull?"

"Well, you're the only other person I know in this school, and you're pretty cool. Didn't want you sitting by yourself."

If it was possible to blush even more, Marie is doing it right now. "Why, thank you."

Great, now I'm blushing. "So, shall we ask each other random questions again?" I break the uncomfortable silence.

"Sure. I don't remember whose turn it is, though."

"I can go. I'll think of something while I chew." I take a bite of my sandwich and think. We've gone through the basic questions for the most part, so I need to be more creative to match the creativity of the person in front of me.

This is going to be fun.

"What's the most embarrassing moment you've ever had?"

Slightly taken aback, she laughs. "Oh man, we're going down the deep end now."

"Well, you didn't state any rules, so I'm asking what I want." I take another bite of my sandwich with a smug smile.

"Oh, man. I don't know," she answers, unsure if she wants to confess. "I have two. One is funny, one…isn't so much. You might not look at me the same way again."

"I highly doubt that. Try me."

"Okay, fine," she relents, taking out a small Snickers bar from her lunch bag before pushing it aside. "I'll start with the depressing one. My ex-boyfriend decided to dump me in a public setting."

Now I'm intrigued. "I haven't dated much, but even I know that's a bad idea."

"Believe me, I know. He called me, we met at a coffee shop and just laid it out on me. Then I started crying, naturally. Then he had the nerve to tell me to be quiet. I wasn't yelling or anything; I was just in tears. It was embarrassing."

Okay, now I'm angry on her behalf. How anyone could do that to someone like Marie, I have no idea. "What a douche," I state pointedly.

"I know. I got up to leave, and he asked me not to make a scene and make him look bad." She swallows hard, trying hard not to cry in front of me. I'm grateful for that, considering I wouldn't know how to comfort a girl that's not my girlfriend. "So I punched him."

I nearly spit out the soda I was drinking. That took a positive turn from dark to highly amusing. "You…punched him?"

"Right in that stupidly pretty face," Marie smirks, taking a bite of her candy bar. "Totally went against what he wanted, and I did make a scene, but I felt a sense of empowerment." She lamely raises her fist in the air. "Girl power."

I have to cover my mouth with my fist to contain the laughter waiting to burst out. "Holy crap, I never thought you were the kind of girl that would punch someone. That's amazing. I have a whole new respect for you."

She rests her chin on her hand and sighs with amusement. "Glad I could entertain you."

"I'm sorry, Marie, I'm not laughing at what you went through," I clarify. "That guy is a class-A dill hole. You showed him."

"Anyway." She shrugs. "Now you know my sob story. Your turn."

"You said you had two. Share them both." I truly want to know more about this girl. Her stories are entertaining.

"I'll tell you after you share yours. Tit for tat."

I start laughing again. "You said tit."

"You are such a guy." She throws a balled-up napkin at me.

"I'm sorry! I couldn't help myself!"

"Of course you couldn't." Marie rolls her eyes. "Now tell me your story."

I have one that immediately springs to mind, but I don't know if I want to tell it. It's not even a huge deal, but I'm still embarrassed it happened. "I can't think of anything. Maybe I just don't embarrass easily."

Marie stares me down with an incredulous look. "You, reclusive Seth Harris, don't embarrass easily? That's unacceptable. You have to give me something."

I feel myself blushing again. "I can't think of one."

"No, you're blushing, I can see it." She points an accusing finger at me. "You have a story. So, what is it? Did you have diarrhea at a girl's house? Fall into a sewer?" She leans in and whispers, "Did you call a vagina a "Virginia" during a sex ed class?"

Marie has made me laugh before, but I can't help the boisterous one that comes out. "You have quite the active imagination."

"Just tell me!" Marie leans forward, ready to listen intently.

I lean back and brace myself. "In middle school, during lunch, I was sitting with some friends. A few tables over, this kid was wearing a cowboy hat, and my friends dared me to flip the hat off his head and bolt. I didn't have anything better to do, so I snuck up to the kid, flipped his hat off his head, and ran for it. He immediately stood up and chased me around the lunchroom. I didn't notice until it was too late that he was about a foot taller than me."

"Oh god," Marie cringes.

"He caught up to me and punched me in the stomach so much that I couldn't move the next day. Everyone in the cafeteria to crowded around and cheered us on. Long story short, we were suspended from school for three days. And we were only into day two of the school year."

"That doesn't sound too embarrassing, though," she remarks.

"That's not the embarrassing part." I hold up my finger in pause. "I bruised so badly that for the next month, people were calling me Peaches."

"Oh yes, I see how that can damage a man's ego."

"Okay, now tell me your next story." Now, it's my turn to lean in and focus my attention on her.

"About a year ago, my best friend Carrie invited me to a game night at her friends' house from her church," she begins. "I think we were playing Apples to Apples or something, and I was laughing so hard I ended up peeing my pants. I tried stopping it, but it just kept going. And it leaked onto the chair I was sitting in. It was a suede chair and beige, so there was a huge dark spot. I didn't even have to pee before that, so maybe my laughing just pushed it out. Anyway, I tried to hide it by taking off my sweatshirt and tying it around my waist because, you know, my jeans got darker. I took a blanket and put it over the chair, then told Carrie's mom what happened."

"Was she mad?"

"Nope. She was actually cool about it. But what made it worse –"

"You sharted?" I guess.

"Oh my god, no, that would be my worst nightmare." She cringes at the thought and then continues, "I came back out to the living room, and one of the girls ended up taking my spot on the pee chair. Carrie's mom said I spilled Mountain Dew on the chair to prevent humiliation. Somehow, it worked."

"Good save. Mountain Dew looks like pee anyway," I mention with a shrug.

Marie gazes at me with what looks like admiration in her eyes. Even adoring. There's nothing to admire about me, and I don't consider myself adorable. At least Tessa finds me attractive, not just physically but mentally. God, I'm so lucky to have her.

I shake my head of my trance. "Okay, your turn to ask a question," I say with my chin propped on my hand, waiting for her.

"I shared two stories. Doesn't that count?"

"You didn't specify the rules of this game, so I say it's your turn," I respond, putting on my most innocent expression.

"You suck." She sticks her tongue out at me, and I return the favor. "Well, since we're getting on the personal side of things, tell me the happiest childhood memory you have."

This isn't just a personal question. It's a deep one. I haven't even gotten this deep with Tessa. That will take time, as she has a hard time opening up about herself. Even so, I continue sharing facts with her, hoping she'll do the same someday.

This is Marie, though. She's my friend, not a girlfriend I'm trying to get to know. So I can share this with her.

"Honestly, it's that car ride," I say, reminiscing about that moment. "It's so simple because it was so fun. And everyone was so happy. It's the last good memory I have of my mom."

I stop talking because I'm about to go down the rabbit hole. I can feel Marie's eyes boring into me, studying me as I relive the memory in my mind. The smiles, the laughter, and the gorgeous views. I would love to have that again.

"Anyway." I clear my throat, getting myself out of that hole. Marie examines me, knowing there's more to say there but also knowing not to push the subject further. "What about you?"

Marie folds her arms with a faraway glance. "I think of the time that my dad hid this toy in his hand, and I tried wrestling it out of his hands, but of course, mine were weak and small because I was, like, six years old. But I just remember laughing so much I peed myself."

"I'm seeing a pattern of peeing your pants here."

"I had a weak bladder, what can I say?" she shrugs. "It's one of the memories I have to keep me from hating him."

That statement makes me freeze. She's another teenager – like me – dealing with anger towards a parent in a divorce situation – like me. Just when I thought I was all alone in feeling the way I did, I found someone who was in the exact same situation.

"You and me both," I state plainly, hiding my shock.

The bell rings then. I didn't realize we had been talking the entire lunch period. I planned to spend the entire time writing in my notebook, but I had more fun talking to Marie.

Marie and I sling our backpacks over our shoulders, and I walk her to her next class, which is right down the hall from the lower level of the cafeteria.

"There's one thing I was wondering," I chip in. "The day we met when you dropped your stuff. You looked like you were having a bad day."

"Oh, I was," Marie confirms.

With this next question, I know I can ask her. We've had deep conversations so far, and I know she will tell me. "Can I ask what happened?"

"The night before," she swallows hard. "It was what would have been my parent's anniversary, and my mom wasn't doing so well, so I was trying to be there for her. Plus, I was still trying to bounce back from everything negative Brad ever said to me about my writing." She pastes on a smile. "I'm doing better now, though."

By the time she finishes telling me that, we reach her classroom. All I can feel is empathy for her. She's such a cool person, yet this ex of hers had the nerve to bring her down. As far as her mom goes, I'm appalled at how strong Marie is to be there for her. I don't know anyone else who would do that for their parents.

Before I can say anything, she turns and grins at me, covering over the deep confession she poured onto me. "I'll see you in sixth period, Peaches."

I roll my eyes. "I knew I shouldn't have told you that story."

CHAPTER 6

Somehow, my body clock wasn't letting me sleep past six on Saturday, so I took a look outside to see what December was greeting us with so far. It's been shockingly cold lately, so I'm not surprised when I open my worn-out blinds to snow covering the ground. Not just a dusting of snow, but inches of it. I even have to put a shirt on. Seeing the snow outside my window made me shiver.

From the looks of it, school will be closed today. The news even confirmed that for me when I turned the TV on, which brought me a sense of relief. There's only one person I want to spend a quiet snow day with, and we have the entire day for it.

"Hello?" Tessa answers groggily when I call her.

"Hey babe, it snowed outside," I speak softly, trying not to wake my dad. I lay back in my bed to shield myself from the cold.

"Oh my gosh, really?" Tessa says excitedly on the other line. I hear her shuffle around and open her curtains to look at the pitch-black outside, the streetlights illuminating the white that covers the ground.

"It's so pretty!" she whispers in awe.

"I knew you'd love waking up to that."

"I do," she says breathlessly. "And you love waking up knowing you won't have to go to school."

"Well, so do you."

"Facts," she says while yawning.

I roll over on my side. "I want to suggest we spend the day together, but I can't drive anywhere with my car."

"My parents have an SUV. I'll come to you."

"But you don't like going anywhere."

"There's not going to be anyone around for what I'm planning," she says, her tone insinuating something that will involve breaking some rules.

I'm all for it.

"Okay, Miss Tessa. Surprise me."

"Wow, it's even prettier with snow," Tessa says when we approach the fence surrounding the Bowl, her gloved hands grasping the chain link and staring in awe. She, of course, is decked out in all-black snow gear, while I have black snow pants, combat boots, and a gray snow jacket.

The football field is completely empty, covered in blinding white powder. The silence around us is almost deafening: no cars, no people, not a peep. It's no wonder Tessa wanted to come here. She loved it when I brought her here on our first date, also at a time when no one would be here.

I shake the gate and find that it's locked. I'm not sure what she planned to do here if we can't even get in. Tessa shows me her plan when she climbs the fence, using the gaps as stepping stones, then plops her feet on the other side.

"Well, come on," she gestures with a frantic wave of her hands.

Mark this as the first day I break into a place when it's closed. I really like this girl, though, and I would do anything for her.

With a shrug, I make my way over the gate, making sure my combat boots don't get stuck in the holes and land on the other side. Tessa takes my hand, and we make our way down the concrete bleachers. The steps are slippery from the ice, so Tessa and I go as slowly as possible. It's not long before Tessa starts to slip, and I grab onto her arm to catch her before she falls.

"Geez, are you okay?" I pull at her arm to help her back up, which was a bad idea because I ended up slipping, too. Pain hits me all at once from the middle of my back to my head when I land on the steps.

"Are you okay?" Tessa bends down to check on me, trying not to laugh.

"I might be broken," I say with a strained voice.

Tessa laughs heartily as she helps me back to my feet. After what feels like an hour, we make it to the football field. I take in the view, appreciating the expanse of white and its reflection on the water out in the distance. A winter wonderland.

Coldness shocks my entire body when Tessa stuffs a handful of snow and shoves it down the back of my shirt.

"Holy crap, that's cold!" I shriek.

"Well, it is snow, Einstein." She sticks her tongue out at me. I retaliate when I bend down and grab a bunch of snow. Tessa takes off running as I ball up the snow in my hand and throw it in her direction. She yelps in pain when it hits her on the back of the head, and she falls over.

"That really hurt!" she whines.

Realizing I probably did something stupid, I trudge through the snow as fast as I can to be by her side. I kneel next to her and lay my hand on her shoulder.

"I'm sorry, babe. Are you okay?" I bend to check on her.

"No," she answers, slightly devious. Before I can react, she grabs a handful of snow beside her and throws it in my face. "Now I'm okay."

"You little –" I tackle her back to the ground. Her laughter and squeals permeate the quiet air, along with the crunch of snow beneath us as we roll around.

Physically tired, we topple over and lay next to each other, breathing heavily. I turn my head to watch her, appreciating this wonderful human who wandered into my life and wondering how I got through life without her in it. I don't know how I lived without that overwhelmingly cute face and petite body. She's made my life worth living.

Tessa turns to look at me and smiles the brightest smile. I scoot closer to her and brush her cheek with my gloved hand before leaning in for a kiss. She wraps her arms around my neck and deepens the kiss. At this moment, I can't imagine being in a better place. I haven't felt this blissful in god knows how long. My heart belongs here with her.

I denied it for a while, but lying next to this girl right now, I've connected my never-ending joy to what I'm really feeling. Over the last few weeks, I can't wait to talk to her every day. The thought of not being near her is like a dropkick to the gut. When I'm near her, the palpitations of my heart speed up so much that I'm surprised it doesn't burst through my shirt. She's constantly on my mind. Her smile, her shyness, her deep brown eyes that flutter every time I kiss her.

I love her. My heart rests solely and completely with her. She makes me feel like I'm on top of the world.

She pulls away and searches my eyes, and her face falls. All her features are downturned when, just a moment ago, she was deliriously happy. It's only for a split second, though, before she lights back up.

"Let's make a snowman!" She springs to her feet, masking what she was just feeling a moment ago, her demeanor switching to a cheery one. I remain on the ground while the sound of crunching snow fades behind me, brows wrinkled in confusion. Something in those deep browns is throwing me off. She seemed almost...sad. Dejected, even. As if it's painful to look at me, because the fun we're having will end.

That won't happen. Not if I have anything to say about it.

WHAT SONG MAKES YOU HAPPY?

Somehow, I knew a music question would come my way at some point.

IT'S A VALID QUESTION!

Fair enough. It's hard to say because it's not just one song. It's a genre of music.

WELL, WHAT KIND OF MUSIC DO YOU LIKE?

Mostly rock. Linkin Park, Pearl Jam, Metallica, Smashing Pumpkins, stuff like that.

ALL GREAT BANDS. WHAT ABOUT NIRVANA? PLEASE SAY NIRVANA *PLACE BEGGING HANDS HERE*

Nirvana's good too. If I had to pick a song, though, I would say Crawling by Linkin Park.

GOOD SONG. LATELY, I'VE BEEN ON AN 80'S ROCK AND SMOOTH JAZZ BINGE.

That's a very random mix of music.

I'M AN OLD SOUL. IT'S WHAT I CONSIDER GOOD MUSIC, AND IT IS AWESOME.

As long as you love it. What about you, music enthusiast?

THAT'S EASY. BLOOM BY MINDI ABAIR.

No clue who that is.

THAT'S BECAUSE IT'S SMOOTH JAZZ. AND SMOOTH JAZZ IS SPIFFTASTIC.

...Spifftastic?

YES. FANTASTIC AND SPIFFY = SPIFFTASTIC.

You are something else, Marie.

Marie stares at my note with a face I can't decipher. Whether she's offended or trying to figure out what to say next, I can't tell. As she thinks, she pulls out her MP3 and headphones from her jacket pocket and plugs them into her ears. Again, I lost track of time. It seems like a full minute before she writes anything back.

I'M WEIRD, I KNOW.

The bell rings after that, interrupting our note exchange. Marie picks a song on her MP3 and leaves the classroom while I follow closely behind her.

Bundled up and ready to face the freezing cold weather of December, I make my way up the steps leading to the courtyard, watching Marie bob her head to whatever music she's listening to. If she wants to show me eighties rock and smooth jazz, this would be a good time.

I tap her shoulder, causing her to flinch in surprise. I hold my hand out, signifying that I want her to share her headphones. She flits her eyes between my fingerless-gloved hand and me for a second. She slaps my hand in a low five.

I laugh at her mix-up. "No, give me your headphone."

She quirks a brow. "Why?"

"You want to show me your 'spifftastic'" – I use air quotes here – "music, now's your chance," I tap my palm with my finger. "Give it up, Katharine Hepburn."

Rolling her eyes, she takes out one of her earbuds and hands it to me. I put it in my ear and look at the screen of her MP3 as I scroll through her song list. "You have the most random mix of music."

"Random? Or spifftastic?" she gives me a dorky smile and a thumbs up for emphasis. Again, there is zero shame in showing her dorky and quirky side.

"I thought you liked the eighties and smooth jazz."

"I do. But I like a mix of everything, too."

"Let's see," I scroll through the artists. "You've got Sarah McLachlan, Kenny G, Van Halen, Def Leppard, and your beloved Mindi Abair, among other artists. Your taste is all over the place."

"It's about the music, not the lyrics. If the music moves me, I have it."

"Apparently, more than one type of music moves you."

"You sayin' that's a bad thing?" she asks with mischief laced in her tone.

"Not at all. I've just never seen such a collection."

"Maybe this will motivate you to add different songs to your collection." She smiles and points her finger at me. "Make it about the music, not the lyrics. Here, I'll pick something you may already know."

She chooses "Come As You Are" by Nirvana, and we make our way down the steps to the parking garage.

"Have you written any more of your story?" Marie cuts in as we slowly make our way to the parking garage.

"I haven't lately," I groan. "But I was thinking about what to write when I get home. I'm still not quite sure how I want the next portion of it to go. I need something to keep readers on their toes; add the shock factor somewhere in there. I just don't know how."

We're in the parking garage now, almost to my car. "Try putting on some music," she suggests. "Pick a song that fits your mood, and something will happen, something that moves you. And I'm not talking about Peter Griffin's obnoxious voice."

"But it's so great," I put on a playfully defeated face.

"If you say so." She grins. "Seriously, switch things up a bit. Just like how people put on music to relax, put it on to get some ideas flowing." She claps me on the arm and takes the headphone out of my ear.

I mull over her words, watching her back away. "I'll try it. Thanks, Marie."

"Let me know how it goes." With somewhat of a sad smile and yearning eyes, she waves and goes back the way we came.

"Your car's over here, Katharine Burn," I call out, pointing my thumb behind me.

She sticks her tongue out at me. "Yes, I know. I'm studying with my best friend at Tully's."

"Overachiever. Have fun."

"Oh, I'll have loads of fun," she replies sarcastically. "Bye, Peaches."

I roll my eyes. "Looks like you found a great nickname for me."

"And I love it," she pumps her fist in the air as she struts off, confidence in every step.

Once I'm on my computer later, I go through the list of songs I have saved on my YouTube account. We're too broke to have Apple Music since each song costs money, so YouTube is music central for me. I added the Nirvana song I was listening to with her to my list.

Marie told me to pick a song based on the music, something that fits my mood. I pick "Shimmer" by Fuel and give it a few seconds to fill my ears. The melody itself is sad. It's the kind of song that can bring a sense of longing. It can force someone to miss what they used to have.

Logged in to Gaia Online, I examine my last post while the song plays. This lost girl in my story can mean something that is important to the main character, something that brings pain and sadness to him.

Something ignites in my mind as the song continues. *All that shimmers in this world is sure to fade away again...*

Ideas are forming. Creativity is blossoming. Maybe, just maybe, the little girl was actually something the main character used to have. Or a girl he tried to save from an accident, but he was too late. She could have been his daughter. The entire thing is a dream that haunts him at night.

Before I know it, I'm typing away on a new post with a smile split on my face. Marie was on to something. Music does help get creative ideas flowing.

Mysterious Snowfield: Part 3

"Can you hear me?" Jason called out again.

The girl still didn't move. Her jet-black hair sways gently with the breeze, becoming a magnet to the tiny snowflakes in the air. It's a miracle she's alive, given her pale complexion.

He can see her lips move, but her words are unintelligible. "What's your name?" Jason asked.

"Home," she said so quietly that he could barely hear her over the whooshing sounds of the wind. "Daddy, I want to go home."

He doesn't quite understand why she's standing there, waiting to go home, when her composure is so calm, like something out of a horror movie. However, leaving her out here in the biting cold was out of the question.

Jason extended his worn and calloused hand. "Okay, I can take you home." He waited for her to take his hand. "Let's go."

She didn't reach for his hand, so he grabbed hers. The moment he touched her hand, though, she disappeared. Vanished.

He twisted slowly in a circle, confused. No one else saw that the girl disappeared but him, so no one could confirm what he had just seen. What is happening? He wondered.

Suddenly, the trees start to vanish, too—one by one. Then, the snow that he's walking through dissipates as well. A black hole below him opened up, and he was sucked into it before he formed his next thought.

Jason shot straight up from his bed, breathing heavily. He looked around his small, dark bedroom, running through the weird dream he just had until his eyes landed on a framed photo of him...and the girl with jet-black hair. That was all the confirmation he needed.

He dreamed about his daughter again. The daughter he misses more than he ever imagined. The daughter he lost.

Holy crap. That took an unexpected turn. And it all stemmed from listening to one song.

Who knew that a song by Fuel would control my emotions, therefore controlling my entire narrative? Even though I had no idea where I wanted the story to go, that little push was all I needed. To add to my surprise, Jason was a good fit for this story. Thanks again to Marie.

Maybe this is a good way to end the story. Leave a cliffhanger for the audience to draw their own conclusions. What happened to his daughter? Is there symbolism involved with being in a snowfield? No one will know.

With that, I post the cliffhanging conclusion to my story. I don't want to stop there, though. I want to keep creating. I want to keep brainstorming and go in another direction. Should I go more romantic? Action? Thriller, like the one I just did?

Adrenaline pumping through my veins from the high of music, I go on YouTube and create a writing playlist.

That's until I receive an IM from Mason.

Mason*: So, what's going on with you and Marie?*

Crap. I didn't see this one coming, to be frank. I didn't think anyone would suspect that Marie and I were anything more than friends. We're friends and friends only. I'm loyal to Tessa, and nothing will change that.

Seth*: Nothing. We're friends.*

Mason*: You've been hanging out with her a lot. You sure you don't have feelings for her?*

Seth*: Absolutely none. You know I'm in love with Tessa.*

Mason*: You're just around her a lot, and you guys seem really comfy together.*

Seth*: I get it. You don't like Tessa.*

Mason*: I don't.*

Seth*: You're the one who suggested getting a girlfriend!*

Mason*: One that would get you out of your hole, not dig you a deeper one!*

Seth*: Either way, I wish you would understand what Tessa means to me.*

Mason*: I get it, but I'm with Victor on this one. Sorry.*

Seth*: Whatever. What's your fascination with Marie anyway? You jumped over her when she dropped her stuff in the hallway.*

Mason*: We have a healthy love-hate relationship. Overall, she's cool. She at least cares about school—something you could use in your life.*

Seth*: Glad to know I have your support, but nothing will ever happen with her. I'm happy with Tessa.*

Mason*: Suit yourself.*

I close out the conversation and lean back in my chair. He had to ruin my feel-good moment by asking about my feelings and criticizing Tessa. Sure, maybe she doesn't help me do better in school, but we're on the same page about life in general, and we get through it together.

That's all that matters to me.

A new message comes through with a *pop*.

Debra: *Will you ever talk to me?*

I groan in frustration and close the message. *Get a clue, Mom. I want nothing to do with you.*

"You look beautiful," I take in Tessa's outfit in my car in front of her school's auditorium. Other students dressed in formalwear and ball gowns make their way through the parking lot, arms entwined with their dates. Tessa's anxiety-ridden eyes roam the scene, ready to back out at any moment. I haven't worn a tux since I went with my mom to see *Phantom of the Opera* in Seattle when I was thirteen. She didn't have anyone to go with, and it wasn't something my dad wanted to do, so I offered to go with her so she didn't feel alone. Granted, it wasn't my thing either, but I loved my mom and wanted to make her happy.

Turned out nothing would make her happier than leaving us.

I take in the girl of my dreams. She's truly stunning tonight. Her hair is curled and held up with a clip, and her makeup makes her eyes sparkle unlike anything I've ever seen, her earlobes decorated with sparkly earrings that hang down just enough to dangle when she moves her head. And her black strapless dress – yes, it's black - reveals her milky white shoulders that I want to bury my neck in later.

God, I love this girl.

"Thank you, you look handsome yourself," Tessa smooths out her dress, eyeing the students arriving at the school. "I mean, you always look handsome." She turns to pat my arm. "Hot, even. So, so hot. I mean, wow, am I a lucky girl!" she laughs nervously and wrings her hands, staring down at her lap. "Sorry, I'm just nervous."

I reach into the backseat and grab a rectangular box. "Well, I hope this helps."

"Oh, you're so sweet," she says, clearly touched by the gesture. "I didn't expect you to get me anything."

"I know. I wanted to." I hand her the box so she can do the honors. She takes the lid off to find a tiara sitting on a pile of tissue paper. It's not a real tiara, but my heart was in the right place. I found it when wandering around the mall with Mason, trying to find a decent tux. I saw it on the wall at the most girly place a guy could go: Claire's. It was Mason's worst nightmare even going into that store, but it was worth every dollar watching him squirm. "You're wasting so much money on that girl," he said when I bought it. Not having a supportive best friend makes this relationship a little harder than I thought, on top of always catering to Tessa's social anxiety.

I never considered myself a romantic person. Ever since I met Tessa, though, she awakened the romantic side of me that I never knew I had. Maybe it had been dormant all this time, and it just took the right person to bring it back to life. Just one more reason to be grateful I met this girl.

"A tiara? Why?" she whispers with shock when she takes it out of the box to examine it.

"I wanted to get you something that wasn't black."

Tessa laughs and grabs my face. "You're seriously the best boyfriend I could have asked for." She kisses me with such intensity that it takes my breath away.

"Ready to dance?" I ask. I'm itching to dance and show off the most dazzling girl in the room.

With a deep inhale, she nods. "I think so."

An hour later, we still haven't danced. At a dance.

No, we're sitting at a table decorated in a white tablecloth away from the crowd, watching everyone else dance. And I'm sure not dancing by myself like a loser.

Tessa's anxiety took over with all the people around; she turned completely rigid, and now we've reached wallflower status. Yes, I'm not a people person, and yes, I'm a lazy bum when it comes to school, but I absolutely did plan to dance with my girlfriend.

Everyone is paired off, having a good time with their silly dance moves and abundant smiles. With the way everyone is dressed, one would think we're at a ball exclusively for royalty. The disco ball twirls above us and shines on the hardwood floor, brightening the silver and royal blue décor that surrounds the place. Fake snowflakes hang from the beams of the ceiling, making it a true winter wonderland theme.

I want to be out there.

"You sure you don't want to go out there?" I gesture to the dance floor.

"I'm okay," she replies sweetly. As much as I'm itching to dance, I would do anything to be loyal to her so I don't put up a fight.

"Hold Me Now" by Thompson Twins starts to play. The itch to dance has become an unbearable urge. She can't say no to dancing to this song. It's the perfect setting for what I'm about to confess to her.

Moving to stand up, I tug at Tessa's arm like a child wanting candy at the store. "Let's dance to this song at least, then we can get out of here. Please."

Tessa's expression reflects the guilt she feels for making me sit with her this whole time, and I'm relieved to see she's going to cave. "Okay," she barely whispers and stands up with me.

My heart races a mile a minute. I'm about to confess my deepest feelings. Not once in my life have I done that. I bring my hand to her hip, take her hand with the other, and sway gently back and forth. Tessa swallows deeply, practically on the verge of a panic attack. Her eyes focus on me with the faintest of smiles.

"Thank you for coming here with me, even if we sat a majority of the time," she says with a smidge of guilt.

Our surroundings fade into the background when I bring myself to pour out my heart to the only girl who holds it in her hands. "There's no place I'd rather be," I say directly into her ear.

"Really?" she questions me, her insecurity breaking through. With her lack of friends and social life and crippling anxiety, she's most likely afraid she'll lose me. Little does she know, I'm not going anywhere.

Instead of answering her right away, I turn to the side and exhale sharply. Nerves crawl all over my body, speeding up my heart. "Tessa. For a while now, I've realized something."

Tessa watches me, anticipating what I'm about to say next. Her eyes hold dread and anticipation, possibly expecting me to break up with her.

I brush a strand of hair behind her ear, locking eyes with her. "I'm in love with you, Tessa."

Her mouth falls open in shock, and tears collect in her eyes. There's a level of sadness there, and I mentally prepare myself for her to tell me she doesn't share the same feelings. Never in my life have I taken a leap of faith like this, and that alone frightens me to no end.

She still doesn't say anything, which makes this a little awkward. Guessing that she's unsure that I'm being serious, I cup her cheek and say with finality, "I love you, Tessa Copeland."

Tears fall down her cheeks, and the widest smile plasters her face when she says, "I love you too, Seth Harris."

My heart explodes into fireworks. "I was worried there for a second," I confess with a chuckle, then I take her face in my hands and kiss her with all the love I have in me. She returns that love with fierce intensity, just the way I hoped.

How my mom turned her back on love is beyond me. Nothing – and I mean absolutely nothing – feels better than this.

CHAPTER 7

Reflecting on the biggest moment of my life has greatly affected my sleep. I'm exhausted, but I don't care.

I'm happy. Ecstatic.

All it took for Tessa to dance with me the rest of the night was for me to confess my love for her. I have never seen her look so joyful. So at peace. Luckily, she remembered to bring a camera to have pictures to look back on to remember this special night. I felt like I was dreaming the whole thing, scared to wake up and find that none of it was real.

All of it was completely real. I told a girl I loved her for the first time. By some miracle, she loves me too.

Life finally feels complete. I finally have something that makes me happy. She and I relate to our need to be introverted, we both have creative minds and don't care about school, and we both feeling like there was a void in our lives. Now we fill each other's void. Sure, we don't help each other improve our education, but we're in love.

My phone vibrates on my nightstand. I slap my hand around and end up knocking over my alarm clock, my phone going down with it. Groaning and not wanting to open my eyes yet, I struggle to fish around for my phone on the floor until I finally find it. I flip it open and answer without looking at the screen to see who called.

Let's be honest; there are only two people who call me, which is Tessa and my dad. Mason prefers using IM to contact me.

"Hello?" I answer sleepily.

"Hey babe," Tessa sniffles, her voice laced with sorrow.

"What's wrong?" My heart races in a panic. She must regret everything from last night. She must have faked everything: the smiles, dancing with me, kissing me, posing for pictures, saying she loves me to make me feel better. Maybe it really was a dream.

"Can you talk?" she asks in a hushed voice.

"Yeah, I can talk." My breathing picks up speed. "What's going on, babe? Are you okay?"

Tessa takes a deep breath, and I brace myself for what she's going to say. "I should've told you this a long time ago, but the thought of telling you tears me up inside, and we were getting closer –"

"Please just tell me, Tessa," I beg her, my heart full on waiting to burst through my chest.

"We're moving in a couple of weeks," she blows through rapidly.

I pause for a second. Okay, she's moving. That's not a big deal, especially if she's not moving far away. That shouldn't affect our relationship that much.

"Okay, well, we can still see each other, right? We can still figure this out. We can still be together," I'm saying more to myself than her. She's crying, though, which means there's more to this.

"Seth. We're moving to Pittsburgh."

With that, Tessa starts to break down in a sob, and I can feel my stomach drop to my butt as I shoot up to a sitting position. I blink a few times and run my fingers through my hair.

Pittsburgh. She's moving to Pittsburgh. As in, on the other side of the country. It's a six-hour flight, at least. This means the odds of seeing her again and keeping this relationship afloat are very slim. With my dad's salary, there's no way I could afford a plane ticket out there. She could always fly back here, but what are the odds her parents would let her do that?

This is what it feels like to have the breath knocked out of you. To be knocked off your feet. I don't want to believe that this is happening. This is the moment where I want to be dreaming.

"Are you serious?" I stutter.

"My dad got relocated for his job," she explains through tears. "I'm sorry, I'm so, so sorry I didn't tell you till now."

"Wait, did you just find out about this?"

Tessa takes a deep, shaky breath. "No. I found out a week after we started dating."

If my jaw could physically hit the floor, that's where it would be. Shock isn't even the best term to describe what I'm feeling. I'm *appalled*. She knew she was moving since we started dating, and not once did she give me advance warning. She had to wait until I gave her my entire heart, only to tell me it was going to be straining.

"A month? And you're telling me this *now*?" I'm practically shouting at her now that I've smoothed out my morning voice from talking to her. I get out of bed in my boxers and pace my messy room.

"Seth, please calm down –"

"Calm down?" Now I'm furious. The audacity of this girl. "We just told each other we love each other. You drop this bomb on me the next day, and you want me to be calm?"

"I was scared," Tessa whines. "I didn't know what would happen to us. I didn't know we would eventually end up at this point in our relationship, so I didn't see the point in saying anything."

She didn't know what would happen to us. How can she say that? We agreed to be a couple after our first date. That would have been the perfect time to warn me that this may not last. My rage is boiling all the way down to my bones. After mom's departure, I didn't think I'd have to face it again. Here I am, my life repeating itself.

After I didn't say anything, Tessa continued, "When I found out, I was actually excited. I thought that maybe starting over somewhere else would give me a fresh start. Make new friends. Not be such a loner. Then we started dating, and I didn't expect it to go as well as it has. Seth, it's been so incredible being with you. Once I knew I was in love with you, it killed me to think about what my life would be like without you. I thought if I ignored the inevitable, maybe it wouldn't hurt so much when the time came when I had to leave."

The sad look she got during the snow day came rushing back to me. The same one she had when I confessed my feelings. She knew she would have to leave me behind soon. She was thinking about how we wouldn't be able to see each other, hold each other, or kiss me anytime she wanted.

I don't have it in me to understand her reasoning. It doesn't help that she had this knowledge the whole time and didn't tell me before my feelings for her got deeper. She had to have known where this was going at some point. We could have come up with some kind of plan going forward.

"Okay, well, we need to form a plan. How long before you leave?"

"A couple of weeks."

If I was furious that she withheld this information before, I'm enraged now. A couple of weeks is not enough time. Not even close.

"You've got to be kidding me!" I yell again, kicking a shelf in my room with my heel. Tessa doesn't tell me to calm down this time. She knows that would be pointless. My breaths are erratic and out of control. Tessa remains silent as I will myself to calm down. She doesn't need the guilt trip right now. She needs reassurance and support.

"And there's no one you can live with? No family?" I plead, grasping at straws at any possibility to make her stay.

"No. All family I have is out of state. Even if I did want to live with someone else, I'd have to start at a new school anyway."

There lies the problem. Her options are limited, and there's nothing I can do. If only I could offer to have her live with me. There is no chance my dad would allow that.

With those limited options, I know one thing. I made her a promise. I plan to keep that promise. We need to make the most of the time we have left before she leaves.

"So, what happens now?" I ask in defeat, sitting back at the edge of my bed.

"Squeeze in as much time as possible before I leave," she proposes weakly.

"And after that? We say our goodbyes, and that's it?" I hate to think that she's entertaining the possibility of ending this relationship. She didn't handle this well to begin with.

"Is that what you want?" Tessa begins to cry again.

"Of course not," I tell her with as much reassurance as I can muster. "I love you, and I want this to work. I will do whatever it takes."

She puffs out a relieved breath. "I love you too. I don't want this to end."

That statement should relieve me, but that doesn't change the thousands of miles of distance that will come between us in the end. She has me wrapped around her finger. "It won't. I promise."

Tessa sniffles. "I know. I never doubted you."

For the first time since my mom left, tears start to well up in my eyes. My body feels like it's been stabbed all over from the inside out. Crippling me. If this is what heartache feels like, then I can't fathom how my dad felt when Mom left us. He probably felt the same kind of pain. It's a miracle he even got through it.

"Let's figure out when to get together, okay?" she says gently.

"Okay, but not right now. I need to process this." *And sulk in bed until I wake up from this god-awful dream.*

"Okay. I love you, Seth."

We say our goodbyes, and I slide all the way to the floor, where I stare blankly at the wall in front of me—specifically, at the spray-painted smiley face who looks drunk. I stare at it in great detail, taking in the ridges and bumps of the drywall as I think deeply about everything from the last few minutes. Tessa wants to make this work. She still wants to be with me. I should be glad about this, but I'm not. Talking through email or phone is not the same as physically being together. I won't be able to kiss her. Hold her. See her smile. Brush back the dark stray hairs that escape from her beanie behind her ear.

This means there's only one solution: a long-distance relationship.

I miss her already, and she hasn't even left yet.

Knock knock.

"No, I'm not looking at naked chicks," I answer before my dad can ask the dreaded question.

Dad saunters in and folds his arms, concerned and serious. He's not even chuckling at his own joke. "Heard you yellin' earlier. Not exactly a good reaction from lookin' at naked ladies."

I don't say anything in response; I just stare at the dead smiley face that taunts me.

"Did she break up with you?" he asks with a glimmer of hope, leaning his shoulder against my doorway.

"She's moving to Pittsburgh." I sigh. "She wants to do long distance."

Dad steps forward and gets down on the floor next to me, leaning against my bed. "Maybe this is for the best, Seth."

"Is that what you said when Mom left?" I snap, and I regret it right away. It's not his fault my mom destroyed their marriage. None of this is his fault. But it bothers me that he doesn't see how happy I've been, that he only focuses on what this relationship wasn't.

"I'm goin' to let that slide because I know you're upset, but next time, those comments won't fly with me," he says sternly. He then turns to face me, pointing a finger in my face. "I want you to listen and listen carefully. Relationships change. Yes, it's painful. It sucks. But sometimes it ends up bein' for the best. Sometimes, it even leads you in a better direction in life. It won't feel that way right now, but you'll look back and see that I was right. It's taken me lots of therapy to figure that out."

Instead of replying to him, I continue to stare at the drunk smiley on the wall. I don't want to accept that maybe he's right. That maybe this relationship is leading me in a better direction in life. I never wanted a different direction. I liked things the way they were. Because life without Tessa is not a future I want to think about; neither do I want to imagine this change in our relationship being for the best.

"Let that sink in," he grunts as he gets back to his feet. "An old man like me can only handle this sitting position for so long. I'm the tin man needin' oil for them joints."

He goes to leave. I have one thing left I want to address, and I hope he will understand. "Dad?"

"Yeah?" he turns back around with a face that says he wishes I did things differently. That look cuts me to the core—every single time.

"I just…" I take a deep breath, my voice sounding more desperate than anything. "I don't want to be like Mom."

When Mom left, my viewpoint on things changed, mostly when it came to potential romantic relationships. She didn't want to work things out with my dad. She was done. At that moment, I promised myself that if I ever found myself in a relationship, I would fight with every fiber of strength I had, and she would have my undivided attention and loyalty.

Dad presses his lips together. "I know," is all he says.

My tires screech when I stop in front of Tessa's house. Moving day came much too soon, and I'm not ready to say goodbye. I will never be ready.

This is the last day I get to see Tessa face-to-face. It's been emotional, to say the least. I had a hard time pretending nothing had changed the last couple of weeks when, in reality, everything is changing. We spent a lot of time packing or just watching movies and eating popcorn. I practically begged to take her out to a restaurant or just a real date in general since I never got to do that with her. Of course, she couldn't bring herself to do that, so we settled for Starbucks, her home space. She felt the need to say goodbye to that place one last time. I got annoyed with how resistant she was to anything that was outside her comfort zone, but I reminded myself of the promise I made and conceded to her wishes.

Mr. Nichol expressed his concern during our last meeting because my grades haven't improved in the last six weeks, and there are about three weeks left of the semester.

I still don't care.

I already know I'm not going to pass any of my classes this semester. Mr. Nichol told me if I don't pass my classes this semester, I would absolutely need to pass next semester so I can graduate with my class. School is the least of my priorities. The women in my life keep leaving, and it keeps tearing me apart.

Tessa races down the steps and down the driveway toward my car; I quickly get out of the car as she crashes into my arms, holding me like I'm her lifeline. In this case, I am.

"I'm going to miss you. So much." I have my arms wrapped tightly around Tessa's waist, rocking her side to side, and tears stinging my eyes.

"I'm going to miss you too," she says through her tears, head snuggled close to my chest. I bury my face in her neck, desperate to hold on as long as I possibly can. She lets go and takes my face in her hands, her brown eyes brimming with sadness. "Maybe I can come back after high school. Find my own place, and we can pick up where we left off."

"I would love that." I nod and stroke her cheek one last time.

Tessa starts to sob. "I love you. I love you so much. You've changed my life in the best way possible. You have to know that."

I grab her face with one hand and kiss her so deeply I have to hold onto her waist to keep her from falling over. "I love you too. So much."

A honk bursts from the SUV, signaling Tessa to hurry and get in the car. I never met her parents because they were always gone when we hung out, but I've concluded that they're a couple of stuck-up snobs. They never even made an effort to talk to me. Right now, for instance, they haven't bothered to get out of their car to say something to me.

Tessa's gaze flits between the SUV and me, almost thinking of just running away from her situation. It would be a dream come true if she decided to stay and found somewhere to live, and we could still be together. Our time is up, though, and there's no way out of it. This is the last time I'll know what she feels like in my arms. The last time I got to feel her lips against mine. The last time I got to hold her hand.

"Let me know when you get there, okay?" I whisper shakily while I kiss her on the forehead.

She nods, then takes my face and gives me a long, deep kiss. We savor the moment to feel everything, prolonging the inescapable reality. We tell each other we love each other again, and she makes her way to the car.

Once they back out and make their way down the street, I run out to the street and watch the car drive my girl and me further and further apart, taking my happiness with her.

Along with my heart.

"Are you okay, bud?" Marie asks worriedly in Microsoft Academy class. "You haven't asked to read my story today, so I know something's up."

We haven't talked much since the whole thing with Tessa went down. No exchanging notes in class, no walking her to her third-period class, nothing. She has reason to be concerned since my behavior has been vastly different. In English class this morning, I was staring off into space, my mind clouded with how I was going to make my relationship with Tessa work. Once the bell rang, I didn't even realize Mason was waving his hand in front of my face, and Marie was watching me with furrowed brows. I grabbed my stuff and left before they could ask questions. Mason is going to ask about it later, and I'm already dreading it. I don't want to talk about it.

I paste on a faint smile, but I don't face her. "Yeah, I'm okay."

She's not convinced, but she doesn't poke the bear. "Look," she whispers, facing her computer. "I consider you a good friend. And as a good friend, I want you to feel like you can talk to me about anything. Okay?"

I almost smile for real. Marie is a beautiful person, inside and out. She's become a good friend. But I can't bring myself to open up. Not just with her, but anyone. I'm back to square one, just existing. I'm going through the motions because there's nothing else I can do. I'm numb inside, just like I was during my parents' split.

"Thanks," I whisper.

We remained silent for the rest of the class. Once the bell rings, we pack up our stuff. My movements are robotic as I grab my backpack off the floor. All I can think about is how much I want to go to bed and lay there. I don't even have it in me to write. Every part of me feels dead.

I hear the clunk and slide of an object coming in my direction, and I turn to see Marie's hand retreat from a Snickers bar that she just handed to me.

"It's my favorite. And it's my last one, so treat it with respect," she teases with a wink.

My lips split into an appreciative smile. "Thanks, Marie," I say while putting it in the pocket of my jacket.

She pats my arm in comfort. "Feel better, okay?" She tilts her mouth up to the side, understanding and sympathy in her expression, and makes her way to the classroom door. She must know I'm not up for conversation since we had been leaving classes together and listening to music the last couple of weeks. A part of me feels guilty because it seems she really wants me to open up to her.

Unfortunately, no one can fix this.

The next morning, I hang out with Mason in the raised brick gardens next to the entrance, writing in my notebook while he studies for finals. Yes, it's that time of year. December is always the month of first-semester finals. The stress and lack of sleep will be palpable very soon for most students.

Last night, I ate the Snickers bar Marie gave me. Snickers are usually not my first choice when it comes to candy bars, but I forgot how good Snickers were. Although it was short-lived, the chocolate/peanut/caramel combination made me feel better about my life.

"Dude, it's cold as balls out here," Mason complains. "Why don't we hang out at the library or something?"

December has shown us how cold it can get. My exposed fingers are going numb; my face is so numb I don't know if it's still attached to my head. However, I know Marie comes in this direction when she gets to school, and I want to switch things up a bit. She brings a sense of positivity and peace to my life, and I really need that right now. Really, I need anything to distract me from the constant ache I have in my chest. I have a whole new attachment I've been feeling with her, and it doesn't want to let up.

"You can go; I'm going to sit out here a little longer," I tell him, my nose buried in the pages of my notebook.

"Suit yourself," Mason mutters while slapping his book shut.

Marie struts across the courtyard, completely oblivious to the world around her, when she bobs her head to the music playing in her headphones. Watching her bask in her happy place, eyes closed, taking in the melody and letting it move her, lights some kind of flame in me.

Backpack in tow, I get up and leave Mason. Mason's voice shouting, "What the crap, dude?" is drowned out by my need to be near Marie. I kind of hoped he would be on his way to the library by the time I left, but I was wrong. I definitely didn't time that well. I pray he just ignores it.

Marie flinches when she sees me, then she greets me with a gorgeous smile and pauses her music. "Hey," she says cheerily but also caught off guard.

"Hey. What are you listening to?"

Marie blinks a few times and stares at me as if she's wondering if I really just followed her into the building. We turn right down a hallway past the office to the staircase right next to it. "ELO," she answers. "'Don't Bring Me Down'."

I hold out my hand for her earbud, as I've been doing lately after school. She hands it to me and lets the song pour into my ears. I understand why she was dance-walking the way she was. It's quite catchy.

"Oh, can I read your story?" I ask for what feels like the millionth time.

Her teeth roll over her bottom lip. "You know what? This might be your lucky day, Peaches."

I stop in the middle of the hallway, delighted and astounded. Her reluctance has finally come to an end. "Are you serious?"

"Yeah." She gets down to her knees and takes her backpack off. "I trust that you're not going to judge me too harshly, so I think I'm comfortable letting you take a look," she says with complete confidence in me. She hands me a folder with a stack of papers in it. If I had to guess, it's probably 120 pages.

"Can I ask what was holding you back?" I investigate.

With a sigh, Marie comes back to standing and tosses her backpack on, eyes aimed at her shoes. "My ex used to criticize my writing," she divulges, her face turning downcast. "He never had a positive thing to say about it, even though he wasn't a writer himself. I would love to get something published one day, but I thought if those are the kind of insults I'll get, I'd rather not share it with anyone. So I've just been writing for myself. You know, therapy," she chuckles uneasily.

Marie hasn't said a lot about her ex, except when she talked about how he dumped her. I didn't like him after that story. Now I just plain hate him. He did everything he could to bring her down. Even though I was never in a relationship before Tessa, I never understood how he could date a girl – a wonderful girl – just to treat her like the bottom of his shoe. The whole point of dating is treating each other the way they deserve. The way they truly feel about each other. That explains her ex's actions. He didn't think much of her and thought everything of himself.

His loss. She deserves better.

"Well, thank you for trusting me," I say with gratefulness as I flip to the first page of her story and start to read aloud. "The sound of pounding hooves in the middle of the night can only mean one thing – trouble.'"

"Oh you don't have to read it right now," Marie says in a panicked tone, her face showing terror. "At least, not out loud."

I narrow my eyes at her, my urge to smile a strong one. "Are you shy, Katharine Hepburn?"

"Hey, it was a big step for me to even give that to you. Don't push it, Peaches," she says, eyebrows raised in a half-serious manner.

"Fair enough," I agree and close up the folder.

I follow her down the hallway to the second-floor stage. The stage is set right in the middle of the second floor of the building, with an open area for seating. The stage curtains are a deep blue with gold tassels on the side, reflecting our school colors, and behind the curtains is a large window that faces the courtyard, bringing in the light from outside. On the third floor, directly above the stage, is a landing where people can look over the gold railing down to the stage.

An olive-skinned brunette girl sits at the edge of the stage, dressed in white tennis shoes, jeans, and a shirt that hugs the curves of her upper body. She studies a textbook on her lap with crossed legs. I've seen her eat lunch with Marie, but I never met her. This must be her best friend.

She lifts her head and sees Marie, then her eyes flit between the two of us, and a knowing smile stretches across her face. A silent conversation occurs between Marie and Brunette as her knowing smile spreads wide. I can't decipher what her friend's expression is saying when her eyes shift to me, but I decide not to spend too much time dwelling on it.

Marie sits next to Brunette at the edge of the stage, and I sit next to Marie. Brunette leans over Marie and extends her hand, showing off all of her pearly whites. "I don't believe we've met. I'm Carrie Moreno, Marie's best friend who will happily punch anyone who hurts her between the eyes."

That forward introduction catches me off guard, but I can't say I hate it. She's obviously very protective of Marie, and I can appreciate that. Marie needs someone in her corner after the heartache she's gone through.

Being the polite guy I am, I shake her hand. "Hi Carrie, I'm Seth." Carrie inspects me, starting with my Converse, then up to my curly head. She gives off the kind of vibe you get when you meet your girlfriend's mom, and you need to make a good impression.

"Nice to meet you. Marie has said wonderful things about you!" Carrie replies with a little too much enthusiasm, which makes me chuckle. She's spunky, hides nothing, and she's protective of Marie. I already like her.

"You can shut up now," Marie implores Carrie through gritted teeth, cheeks turning a dangerous shade of red. She's been talking about me. Why would she want to talk about me to her best friend? Given that she's embarrassed, the only conclusion I can come up with is that she has feelings for me, which I doubt is happening. Marie hasn't told me she has feelings for me, so that can't be it. She's bubbly and happy with just about everyone around her. She's not singling me out.

No, no feelings there.

"I would normally ask you questions and get to know you, but finals are driving me up the wall, and I have to study," Carrie points out, plopping the textbook back on her lap as Marie flops back on the stage and lays there, plugging in her headphones. "But it was nice to meet you, Seth," Carrie adds with a wink.

"Oh yeah, you too," I reply before she goes into full-blown focus mode. I flop on my back to lie next to Marie as she listens to her music and gazes at the high ceiling. I hold out my hand, my cue for her to give me an earbud. She takes one out of her ear and hands it to me. There were some saxophone sounds coming out of it before she changed it to something else.

"Wait. Go back to that song."

"It's smooth jazz. I don't want to torture you with that."

"It's okay. You wanted to show me the spifftasticness of smooth jazz. Let's hear it." I give her a reassuring grin.

The smile on her face is appreciative. "Okay, but you can't judge me if you don't like it."

"Which song are we listening to?"

"Bloom. Mindi Abair."

As the strumming of the guitar introduces the song, I study Marie as she looks back at the ceiling. It occurs to me that, under the confident exterior, she's insecure. She worries about what people think of the things she likes. It makes me sad for her because she shouldn't care. No one should make my Marie feel that way.

Wait. *My* Marie? No. Marie. Just *Marie*.

Once I get that into my head, I focus on her favorite song. The saxophone melody begins, putting the guitar in the background. No lyrics, just the smoothness of a saxophone blending in with drums and guitar. I haven't reacted quite yet since I don't know how I feel about jazz music. It never appealed to me, so I never gave it a chance.

As the song progresses, it gives a hopeful tune, as if you're about to reach the top of a peak you've been trying so hard to reach, and then it crescendos into the chorus, like the victory has been claimed. I must say, Mindi Abair has some serious talent. She has the miraculous ability to bring emotion to life.

Marie's eyes mist with unshed tears. Watching her react this way, I finally understand why she's plugged in all the time. Music means something to her. It speaks to her. It pulls her out of the muck of her own emotions. I can see why. Thanks to her, it affected my writing in ways I didn't anticipate.

When the song is over, she sniffs and shakes her head to rid herself of any emotion, hiding how the song made her feel. She grabs her MP3 and gives me an evil grin. "Now, for the naughty side of me," she says and shuffles through her song list.

Now, she has me extremely curious. I knew Marie had somewhat of a wild side, but I wanted to know what her definition of "naughty" was.

My question is answered when I suddenly hear the song start with, "Oh. My. God. Becky, look at her butt. It is so. Big."

No way. She has *this* song on her MP3 player? She *likes* this song?

That is...comical.

This song is so out of the ordinary for Marie, who's been into the more innocent songs.

When the beat starts, Marie's head swivels around, and laughter plays at my lips. I'm frozen in place and still listening because I can't believe Marie has "Baby Got Back" in her music list. She's totally into it, moving her arms and head to the beat.

When Sir Mix-A-Lot says, "I want to *grunt* double up," a full-on belly laugh makes its way out.

"What's so funny?" she asks while holding back a laugh.

"I know you only focus on the music," I begin when regaining my composure, "but you realize this song is about...boning people, right?"

Marie sits straight up, laughing uproariously, and then it quickly morphs into full-blown hysterics. So much so that she's hunched over, face beet-red. Even Carrie looks over at us with a perplexed look. "What's so funny?" she mouths.

I really don't know. The only thing I know is my brain has stopped listening to the music, and now all I hear is that boisterous laugh. She's laughed in front of me before, but not like this. Pride courses through me, knowing I caused that to happen. The contagious sound causes me to laugh along with her again. Marie is a beautiful girl, but seeing her like this makes her breathtaking.

After she calms down, she gestures with her hand when she states, "As I said, it's about the music, but now I know I can count on you to point out that a song I have is about...boning people."

She lets out another fit of laughter. Now I know that's what makes her laugh like this, along with using terrible accents to talk to each other. Make a note of that for future use.

"Take a chance, take a chance. He's not Brad. Be a new flower," Marie repeats to herself at just above a whisper in Microsoft Academy class.

Marie has never been one to talk to herself. There must be a reason for this.

"What?" I ask and turn towards her.

Her cheeks turn a bright shade of pink. "Sorry. I was just praying."

I chuckle and turn back to my email, where I'm checking for any new messages from Tessa. It's been a week since she moved, and I haven't received any emails from her. I've called her and left voicemails, but she hasn't returned my calls. I can only guess she's been swamped with getting settled with a new life and new changes.

From the corner of my eye, I can see Marie watching me as she has an internal debate with herself. I never told Marie about Tessa. It just never came up. I also never said anything to Tessa about Marie. Tessa is already an insecure person; I didn't want her feeling worse and doubting our relationship, even though she has nothing to feel insecure about.

Marie finally clears her throat and whispers, "So, are you doing anything before school tomorrow?"

I shake my head, my brows pinched together. My morning routine consists of hanging out with Mason outside or going to the library. I'm not usually one to change my routine. "No. Why?"

"I was wondering if you, um..." she swallows hard, then finishes in a rapid breath, "if you wanted to get coffee at Tully's with me tomorrow."

I pause, unsure of what to do. My emotions are teetering between guilt and a desire to enjoy life. When I got coffee, it was always with Tessa. That became our tradition throughout our relationship. It seems wrong to start that up with someone else. What's worse is, from the way it sounds, Marie is asking me out on a date.

Marie and I have never expressed that kind of interest in each other. We get along really well, and I laugh more than I ever have in my life with her, but that's all it is. There has never been anything romantic between us. Besides, I really need the company of a good friend to get me through this.

"Sure, that sounds good," I answer, lips quirked in a smile.

Marie's entire body relaxes, and she breathes out in relief. "Okay. Okay. Cool. Do you want to just meet me at the S in the courtyard?"

"Yeah, sounds good."

The bell rings, and Marie plugs in her headphones. We walk out the door and up the stairs to the courtyard.

"What are we listening to today?" I hold my hand out. Apparently, asking me out to for coffee was a nerve-wracking moment for her, and I need to put her at ease.

Especially if we're going on a date/not date tomorrow morning.

Without a word, she grins and picks "Armageddon It" by Def Leppard. It's a fun song to rock out to on the way to the parking garage.

Screw it. I want to enjoy life. So I'm going to enjoy life.

CHAPTER 8

Tessa: I miss you.

The picture she sent me through IM makes me so happy. She's waving at the camera in her new bedroom with a slight smile, but no beanie in sight. It's a new look for her, and it's refreshing to see that side of her. Man, have I missed her.

Seth: I miss you too, babe. You look beautiful.

I should be in bed by now, but I haven't talked to Tessa in what feels like years, so I will do whatever it takes to make sure I talk to her, even if I stay up late. If we keep up with these nightlong conversations, I'm going to turn into a zombie.

She's worth it.

Tessa: Thank you. Figured I would change things up a little.

Seth: How are you feeling?

Tessa: Ugh! Exhausted. I can't seem to get over this time difference. And I can't get over not seeing you like I used to. I don't like it.

The ache I've been feeling since she left is making a raging comeback. I feel the same way she does with this whole thing. This is the hand we were dealt, and we both want to stay together, so I'm going to see this through. It would take the Lord Jesus himself to come from heaven and tell me to dump her for me to give up on this relationship.

Seth: *We got this, Tess. I'm still in if you are.*

Tessa: *I'm still in, too. We got this. I'm just scared.*

Seth: *Me too. But I'll always love you.*

Tessa: *I love you too, babe.*

A twinge of sadness hits me. I'm glad we still have hope, but it means we have to put in the effort apart. I don't know how my dad managed to survive this heartache.

Nevertheless, Tessa's still in, and that's all I'm going to focus on.

I trudge up the steps from the drop-off area, one step at a time. I'm absolutely not in the mood to be here. That's usually how I feel anyway, but I'm feeling it to the absolute max. Marie wanted to get coffee with me, though, and I don't want to cancel on her.

At the center of the courtyard, Marie stands there with her winter jacket and a beanie that Carrie is fixing up for her and stuffing her hair inside of it. Carrie sees me approaching, and she turns and runs off in a frenzy, leaving Marie in the cold.

Marie manages a smile that masks her anxiety. "You okay, bud? You look tired."

She's right. I am freaking exhausted.

"Oh yeah, I'm fine," I say nonchalantly. I tilt the corner of my mouth in a weak smile, but it's far from reassuring.

She pats me on the arm. "Okay. Maybe a cup of coffee will wake you up."

We make our way to North 1ˢᵗ Street, where Tully's waits for us at the top of the hill. A harsh exhale forms a cloud in front of my mouth as I attempt to wake myself up. I'm not sure what caused Marie to ask me to get coffee with her, but she seemed edgy. Extremely edgy. We're usually very comfortable around each other, so I'm not sure where this new behavior is coming from. It's just getting coffee, as friends.

As we walk up the hill, taking our time, I notice Marie is abnormally silent. I glance at her at the same time she turns to face me, then blushes and turns her head away.

This isn't an awkwardness I'm used to. We've been asking each other random questions since we met, but my mind is completely blank from lack of sleep. She's clearly uneasy, and yet my ability to put her at ease is useless. For some reason, it took a mountain of courage for her to invite me.

"So, I've been wondering something," Marie breaks into my whirling mind with her sweet, inquisitive voice.

"Uh oh," I reply warily. When someone starts a conversation with that, it's usually a segue into a serious discussion.

"It's not bad," she assures me. "I just know you don't do homework or anything in class except write in your notebook. I was just wondering why. Do you not like school?"

I suppose I should've expected her to ask that at some point. It's not like I hide the fact that I do nothing in any of my classes. I just don't like having this conversation with anyone. Because it largely involves my mom.

"If you don't want to talk about it, its fine," she backpedals after the brief silence between us, cheeks turning pink. "I mean, we've shared some personal things before –"

"No, no, it's a valid question." I debate with myself how much I want to divulge to her. How much of myself should I reveal because the truth of it all is embarrassing. So, I share part of my truth. "I don't know. I would just rather write. I like to live in a character's reality, apart from my own."

"I understand. I would rather write than do homework too. But I have a feeling there's more to it than just wanting to write." She taps the side of her head with her finger. "There's more going on up there."

Man, she's perceptive. I'm debating on how much I want to divulge. I really don't want to tell her about Tessa. That will just result in her distancing herself from me. I like having her next to me. I *need* her next to me.

"I guess I don't see the point anymore," I admit with slouched shoulders.

Marie's face contains such compassion that it burns a hole in my chest. "What do you mean?"

Sighing, I press the crosswalk button. Marie waits for me to elaborate, ready to listen. "My mom always talked about the importance of working hard for things that matter, especially education. She had high hopes that I would go to a good college. Then she, um," I swallow through the ache of telling this truth, "Switched teams. Left us in the dust. I kept thinking, what value is her advice if she ended up leaving us behind?"

"Wait." She holds up a hand in pause. "What do you mean she 'switched teams?'"

I harshly exhaled. This is the part I hate talking about. "Let me put it this way. She decided she didn't like...men. Anymore."

"Oh," Marie breathes out softly, thinking about what I just said. Then, her face lights up in understanding. "Oh!"

The light turns, and we proceed to cross the street. Marie grabs my arm in comfort. "I'm so sorry, Seth. Were you guys close?"

"Yes. We talked about everything. Now we don't talk at all. She tries reaching me all the time, but I'm still too mad to talk to her, so I ignore her."

She nods and breathes out, processing that heavy load I just dumped on her. "I get it," she consoles me. We get to the entrance of Tully's, and she stops me in front of the door, hand on my chest as she speaks. "I really do. One thing I've learned from avoiding my dad is that, deep down, neither one of us wanted to keep living that way. I was mad at him, ignoring him when he would try to reach me. It could only go on for so long. So, recently, I decided to start talking to him again."

"And how's that been going?"

A satisfied smile spreads across her face in a tight line. "It's been good," she tells me. "In fact, it's been nice." She shrugs. "I mean, he's my dad. I still love him."

She walked into the café and opened the door for me to enter with her. I stood there for a moment, thinking about the silent message she was sending with that story. In a way, that message was "talk to your mom."

"As far as school," she continues, "there's a sense of accomplishment you feel when you put in the work versus when you don't. Think about what you want your end goal to be, and put your mom's advice to good use. Be the one that proves to her that you're not letting her bring you down. Just because she left doesn't mean her words have no value."

Accomplishment. Is that what my dad and Mason have been trying to tell me when they say I need to find something that motivates me? So I can feel accomplished? I thought finding Tessa was the happiness I was seeking. I am happy. She didn't help me accomplish anything with my education, but I was in complete ecstasy with her.

I examine the sincerity and empathy emanating from Marie. A part of me is glad I opened up to her. I don't usually do that, but she's so approachable and kind. The way she studies me with those bright green eyes that sparkle with interest, how perceptive she is when something isn't right, and her need and desire to help. She makes it so easy to talk about the deeper things.

Then it hits me. I have never shared that tidbit about my mom with Tessa. My own girlfriend doesn't know that vital piece of information. She never asked. All she knows is that my mom left. My friendship with Marie is deeper than my romantic relationship with my girlfriend. Something isn't right with that.

We were never really the kind of couple that shared those kinds of facts with each other. Her lack of a social life, her artistic brain, and her rambling when she was nervous were the things that drew me to her. She was never one to really go deep into her history. Everything was more surface-level. I was okay with that. I *wanted* to be okay with that because we became each other's security blanket. I was the security she never had.

"Is that why you work so hard? Because you see the end goal?" I ask, turning this conversation to her.

"That and I just want to get it over with," she states. "I want to graduate and be done with it. I've had to deal with my parents' split and a humiliating breakup within a six-month span, so I've thrown myself into schoolwork and writing, just so I don't have time to think about any of it."

I have never felt sorrow this intense for someone. Marie – sweet, funny, and kind Marie – doesn't deserve to struggle. She deserves all the good things life has to offer.

Including a guy who will treat her the way she deserves. She's broken inside, yet she smiles and seems to exude positivity while that pain hangs in the background of her mind.

Marie Katharine Burn is a strong woman.

"I'm sorry," I manage to choke out.

"It's okay," she gives me a half smile, one that says she appreciates the sentiment. "Have you thought about talking to a therapist?"

"No," I scoff. "I hate the idea of seeing a therapist."

"If you're worried it makes you look weak, that's where you're wrong," she points out. "Maybe you should give it a shot."

"What about you? Would you give therapy a shot?" I fire back.

"Writing and music are my therapy. I'm set," she winks, then points a finger at me. "You, sir, should try therapy. And talk to your mom."

I chuckle. "Giving me assignments, Katharine Burn?"

"Yes," she juts out her bottom lip and lifts her chin up with playful indignation. "Make a note for yourself" – she takes her finger and writes in the air – "Therapy session for Peaches."

I hang my head and laugh at the ridiculousness of it. "That sounds like an appointment for a cat."

A barista approaches us while we're mid-laughter and asks her what she wants. "I'll get a hot chocolate and banana bread, please," Marie says with a jovial lilt.

This takes me back to my first date with Tessa and her complicated coffee order. And all the complicated orders she placed every time we went to Starbucks after that. I can't help but compare that to Marie's order. It's simple. She doesn't need the unnecessary ingredients. She's content with the basics.

I like that. A lot.

"Do you want anything?" Marie turns around to ask me.

Normally, I'd get a hot chocolate, but I'm still trying to wake up, and I'm not in the mood. "No, I'm good."

The barista gets to work, and Marie turns to me with a surprised expression. "You didn't want to get anything?"

"I'm okay," I shrug.

"You endured this arctic weather just to watch me get a hot chocolate?" She's amused but also feels sorry for me.

I don't regret it. Not one bit.

"I wanted to," I tell her. "I enjoy your company."

My mind does a record scratch. I don't know what it is about Marie and being around her, but I've been deep and honest this entire friendship. It's...different. Freeing.

Marie gazes at me with such appreciation in her sparkling green eyes that I get lost in them. "Well, thank you," she says, cheeks reddened.

She clears her throat and turns to the barista who just put down her hot chocolate and banana bread, then I follow her out of the coffee shop. I look at the spires of Stadium High School down the hill, and I feel depressed. I don't want to go back to school. I want to sit with Marie at Tully's and talk. Chill out. Which is a scary feeling because I haven't felt that way since I started seeing Tessa.

Wait. Why am I thinking like that?

Tessa. You're in love with Tessa. Your loyalty is with Tessa. *Repeat that mantra, and you'll be fine.*

Once we get to the stoplight, Marie takes her first sip and nearly spits it out. "Oh. Wow. That's hot."

"But how does it taste?" I ask while we cross the street.

She opens and closes her mouth to relieve the heat. "I'll let you know when my tongue stops burning."

I chuckle and lend out my hand. "Mind if I try it?"

Marie takes her gloved hand and wipes the lip of the cup off. "There. No kooties."

"I can handle kooties, especially your kooties," I respond. Marie's examines me, trying to see if I was flirting or just making a statement.

Am I flirting?

Our close friendship has made me say things I never thought I would say to a girl. By the looks of it, those things are hitting her differently than most conversations we have. It's kind of adorable.

Tessa. You're in love with Tessa. Your loyalty is with Tessa.

We make our way down the hill, and I bring the cup to my lips and take a sip. I barely manage to swallow the sugary liquid chocolate. "Okay, yeah, that's hot."

"Did you think I was kidding?" Marie laughs with her hands spread out.

"A part of me wondered if you were just a weenie," I joke and hand her back the cup.

"I could easily pour this all over your lap and claim you have incontinence issues." Marie challenges me with those gorgeous eyes that could pierce into my heart. She holds her cup out to me. "Hold this while I get some Depends for you."

"You play dirty, Marie Katharine Hepburn."

"God, I never should've told you my middle name. Peaches."

Just in the last twenty minutes of being with Marie, my mood is exponentially better.

Hey babe,

I miss you! We've been so busy unpacking, and it's been exhausting. How's your day going so far? Love, Tessa

I checked my email in Microsoft Academy class and found this unread message, and immediately I'm consumed with a guilty conscience. I have this wonderful girl in my life, and I went to get coffee with another girl. It felt like a date. I shouldn't be on "dates" with other girls. I should be on dates with my girlfriend.

Tessa's message is also short, which is somewhat disconcerting. I make the excuse that she's probably just tired, and adjusting to a brand new city, state, and school is overwhelming. I will myself to calm the panic in my chest that begs me to believe she doesn't love me anymore.

If I've learned anything from my parents' divorce, it's that honesty is extremely important in a relationship. And if I want to maintain my loyalty to Tessa, I should probably be honest with her. I've held back long enough at this point.

I click Reply and start a message.

Dear Tessa,

Since we talked last night, I wasn't in the best mood this morning, but I'm doing much better. I miss you a lot, Tessa. You consume my thoughts every day. I miss hearing your voice. Can we talk on the phone tonight?

So, I never told you this because it wasn't important, but I feel that you should know. Around the same time I met you, I met this girl named Marie. She's in a couple of my classes. We've become good friends, exchanging writing ideas and such. She invited me to get coffee with her this morning before school, and she seemed nervous about asking me so I didn't want her to feel bad, so I agreed. It was fun, but I also felt guilty. I don't know if it was a date or just friends getting coffee, but I just wanted to tell you because I want to be honest with you. Always.

I love you so much, Tessa. You have no idea.

Love, Seth

I sent the email and waited anxiously for her reply. With the time difference, it's probably almost evening over in Pittsburgh. She should be glued to her computer, waiting to talk to me.

After pretending to do actual work, I check my email again. Nothing.

That's unusual. She usually responds right away.

I continue to browse Gaia Online for another twenty minutes, then check again. Still nothing.

As I will myself to calm down, the bell rings, and I walk out with Marie as usual and listen to "Chill or Be Chilled" by Oli Silk playing in my ear. I feel like the dynamic between us has changed now that we have had some one-on-one time outside of school.

"End of semester party at my house!" I hear a girl's voice announce in the hallway when I walk in to meet Marie at the second-floor stage, only to find she and Carrie aren't there. In the hallway, I see them each carrying a stack of invitations and handing them out to select students. "No booze or drugs, or I will cut you!" Carrie barks out with the seriousness of a drill sergeant, then puts on a cheesy smile. "Jesus loves you!"

Standing at the end of the hall, I watch Carrie and Marie have a deep conversation as students take invitations from their hands. Some look at Carrie like she's gone mad and walk past her. I don't blame them. Carrie's a feisty one. Marie, on the other hand, has the stance of someone who wants to be somewhere else.

I can't say I've ever been to a high school party. It's never really been my scene, considering that they get crazy with alcohol and experimenting with drugs. Mason usually never went either, so we'd end up going to each other's houses and playing video games. We also weren't the kind of people that were invited to parties. However, Carrie said there would be no alcohol or drugs, so maybe I could check out my very first high school party. A big plus is that Marie will be there. Someone I can hang out with.

I approach them as Carrie is whispering to Marie. Marie sees me, and her eyes widen. Carrie turns to me in the middle of a sentence and says in a high-pitched voice, "Heeeeey, Seth!"

"Hey," I greet them incredulously.

"Marie and I would love to have you at my end-of-semester party at my place," Carrie announces with a cheerful lilt and hands me an invitation.

"If you don't want to, it's totally fine –" Marie starts to say. Out of nowhere, Carrie gently elbows her right in the stomach to get her to stop talking.

"Believe me, she would love to have you," Carrie cuts in with a wiggle of her eyebrows while Marie grunts and doubles over. Whatever is going on between them must have something to do with me. They're both acting suspiciously strange.

"Thanks, I'll think about it," I reply with questions in my mind when I glance between Marie and Carrie, then make my way down the hallway.

"Hope you can make it!" she calls out to me. "Marie would really, *really* like to see you!"

I ignore Carrie's voice and study the invitation. The party is days after the semester is over, which will be a nice start to winter break. There's also the possibility that I won't have any classes with Marie next semester. Which means I will see her less. Note-passing will be a forgotten trend, along with listening to music from her MP3 player.

The thought of that ending is a sense of loss I don't want to experience again. I can't stand losing someone else who's become very important to me and has helped me in so many ways.

There's only one thing I can do to prevent that from happening.

When I get a chance in Microsoft Academy class, I get out a piece of paper and write a note for Marie.

```
I would like to keep in touch since I don't know if
we'll have classes together next semester.
555-1969
wannabepetergriffin@yahoo.com
```

Before I give it to her, I peruse the note, giving myself the chance to back out. She will be the only other girl besides Tessa that I will be communicating with. Oddly enough, I find myself feeling okay about it. My conscience is clear. Tessa knows I talk to Marie. This is okay.

I lay the note on her keyboard. I pretend to work while she opens the paper, and the broadest of smiles begs to cross her lips, but she holds back. She's excited. As in, *very* excited. I'm just giving her my number so we can talk during the next semester. I don't see the big deal.

I watch as she puts the contact information in her cell phone, then writes a response and slides the note back to me.

That would be great!
Caddyshack@msn.com
555-2775

Oh, thank god. She wants to keep in touch with me, too. I can't help but chuckle at her email, though.

Caddyshack?

I KNOW IT'S WEIRD. I REMEMBER HEARING IT SOMEWHERE AND THINKING THAT IT WOULD BE A GOOD EMAIL TO HAVE.

Maybe because it's a popular 80's movie?

...THAT WOULD EXPLAIN IT.

I chuckle at her response and stuff the note in my jacket pocket for safekeeping. All I'm grateful for now is that I'm not going to lose someone else in my life.

No new messages from Tessa.

This is odd. Her behavior is very different from when we first started dating. I have a very subtle but nagging feeling that Tessa's slipping away from me. For someone who feared me leaving her, she's doing exactly that to me.

No. That can't be right. She wouldn't leave me. She doesn't have it in her to do that.

I get up from my chair and search my gray jacket for the note with Marie's phone number. I should check to make sure it works. I would hate to call it next semester, only to have it be wrong.

Okay. Fine. I want to talk to her.

The odd thing is, I'm not even tense. The first time I talked to Tessa on the phone, I was a bundle of nerves. Somehow, all is calm. Maybe because there's no romantic interest in Marie. She's basically one of the guys.

"Hello?" her sweet voice answers after I dial her number.

"Hey, it's Seth." My voice comes out gruff and sexy, just like the way Tessa liked hearing my voice when we first talked on the phone. "What are you up to?"

"Well, I was talking to Carrie on IM, and before that, I was studying for my last final."

"What were you guys talking about?"

"Just stuff," she says with indifference. "She's usually the person I go to when I need help with homework. Once in a while, I'll ask Mason."

"Mason's a nerd, so he would be a good choice."

"Which I use to my advantage," she counters. "Hey, have you read my story yet?"

God, I'm such a sore loser. With Tessa on my mind, writing my own stuff, and forgoing sleep most of the time, I haven't been in the right mindset to pick it up and focus on it. Marie deserves more than a half-hearted focus on her work, so it sits safely on my desk, begging me to open it.

I clear my throat. "I haven't. Been busy."

"With what?" she inquires, her tone borderline insulted. "You watch *Family Guy* and write online. You asked me for weeks to read it."

"I know, I'm sorry. I will get to it, I promise," I tell her. Not wanting to talk about how much I've failed her, I ask, "What quote do you think Miss Buhler will write on the whiteboard next?"

Seemingly thrown off, she clears her throat and stammers a bit before saying, "I don't know. Maybe something about loving your cats."

"You and your obsession with cats."

"Hey, cats are great, and you know it."

"You don't even have a cat!"

"Unfortunately, no." Her voice lowers in sadness. "We did have a cat when I was a kid, though, but we had to put him down. He had a large tumor in his stomach."

"That sucks. What was his name?"

"Tic-Tac. He was all white and looked like a Tic-Tac."

"Tic-Tac," I repeat to myself. "I like it. Let me guess, you named him?"

"Who else?" she proudly states. "When I become a CCL, I will name my cats proudly."

"I don't doubt it."

"Hey, I'll talk to you later," she suddenly tells me, and I hear a woman's voice in the background. "I've been summoned by my mother."

"Okay. Have a good night, Marie."

I can hear her smile when she says, "You too."

As I write in my notebook, I hear a couple of *pops* from my IM. Praying that it's Tessa, my head shoots up to my Instant Messenger. One message is from someone I don't want to talk to, and the other is my best friend. My heart plummets.

Debra: *Just checking in to say hi. I miss and love you.*

This would be a great opportunity to take Marie's advice to heart and respond to her. I can't bring myself to do it. The burning anger I feel deep in my chest still burns brightly. I'm not as good and thoughtful as Marie.

I deleted the message and opened the one from Mason.

Mason: *Hey bro, are you going to Carrie's party? Marie is begging me to be there, and she's the only person I know who's going. And maybe Harmony. I need my wingman!*

Shoot. The party is this weekend. I almost forgot. The finals are over, so Carrie scheduled it right when people would want to let loose. I never decided if I wanted to go to Carrie's party or not. My mood is pointing in the direction of staying home and waiting for Tessa to respond to me. I miss her like crazy.

There's going to be a ton of people at this party, and that fact doesn't appeal to me. However, Marie will be there. I would be lying if I said I wasn't curious about what she would be wearing for the theme. Something other than her typical skater shoes and ponytail. A dress, maybe. One that clings to every part of her curvy body —

Knock knock.

"You lookin' at naked chicks in there?" my dad bellows from the other side of the door. Again, with the dumb question.

"No," I groan.

Dad's broad shoulders enter my open door and nods at my computer. "What are you doin'?"

He asked me that often during finals. He played it off like he was checking on my well-being when he really wanted to see if I reconsidered and focused on finals, which I didn't. I already knew I wasn't graduating, so I didn't see the point. Dad is close to giving up on encouraging me to do better.

"Just writing and talking to Mason," I reply.

He leans closer to my screen and squints to read Mason's message. "You were invited to a party?" I turn to face him, and he's legitimately stunned. "You were invited to go out and socialize? As in, you have friends that want to hang out with you?"

I narrow my eyes at him. "You make it sound like I don't have friends."

"That's because you don't. You live like a nun." He points at me. "You're goin' to that party. You need to get out of this house and stop mopin'!"

"I have not been moping!"

"Oh, don't give me that crap," he scolds. "That's all you've been doin' since that *girlfriend* of yours moved. Please, for the love of all that is holy, go to this party. In fact, I'll drive you there Friday night and make you spend the night, so you *have* to go!"

With the way I ended this semester, it's abnormal for him to suggest I go to a party. He wasn't suggesting it before winter break, which means he has an ulterior motive.

He wants me to let Tessa go.

That's been the source of my frustration lately. He understands my need not to ditch Tessa, but he doesn't approve of her impact on my life. For once, I wish he would focus on why I love her.

I turn back to my computer screen, Mason's message glowering at me for an answer. With the amount of people that snagged an invitation to the party, it's going to be so crowded it will be suffocating. I'm not used to being around that many people. I only went to Tessa's dance to be with Tessa and to dance with her, not to have sticky, sweaty bodies squishing me.

Mason plans on going, it seems. Marie will be there, as she is hosting the party with Carrie. I could just stick with them the whole time. If there's dancing, that's an added bonus. Besides, I really don't need my dad to take me to Carrie's house before the party. Talk about weird.

"Okay, I'll go," I surrender. I'll go for Mason's sake. He needs a wingman, and he's my closest guy friend. That's the only reason.

Dad's expression softens as he raises his arm in the air and cheers then turns to exit my room. "Atta boy! You're goin' to have a blast!"

I heave a sigh when he happily struts down the hallway. I turn back to my computer and type a reply to Mason.

Seth: *Yeah, I'll be there.*

CHAPTER 9

The music is bumping. It's so loud, I'm sure aliens in Jupiter can hear it. That's the one sign I have to tell me I'm in the right area in the darkness of the night, besides the cars parked all along the street.

For an 80's and 90's themed party, something in me wanted to dress to impress. With a leather jacket, form-fitting dark wash jeans, a black t-shirt that clings to my entire torso, and Converse, I put on the bad boy persona. I wasn't going to change my shoes. I'm still technically going with the theme there. I also straightened my hair, something I haven't done in years. I never even did it for Tessa. She has no idea what my hair looks like when it's straight.

Walking up the slight incline of the driveway, I feel a mix of anticipation and anxiety ignite in my body. People hang out in random spots on the lawn, either sitting in the grass or standing, talking and laughing. I don't know how people can stand out here. It's at least thirty degrees outside.

I answer my own questions when I walk through the front door. The house is packed with a sea of bright-colored leggings, big hair, afros, bell-bottoms, and a cat costume – what in the world? – and knee-high socks. The variety here is immense.

"I Can't Wait" by Nu Shooz booms throughout the house. People crowd in the kitchen towards the back of the house, getting snacks and drinks. There's a giant stereo in the living room on the left, and to the right are stairs that lead to a basement level downstairs and to bedrooms upstairs. All the windows and doors are open – thank god – because it's extremely stuffy in here. I turn towards the living room and find Carrie with her arm propped up on the monstrous speaker in front of the fireplace, with a wooden sign on the mantle that says, *"As for me and this household, we will serve the Lord."* With the way this party is raging, Carrie is a walking contradiction to those words.

Carrie sees me and waves. She's wearing a short, red plaid skirt with a tight white shirt, with her hair curled, bright red lipstick, and black stilettos. Again, this is a walking contradiction to her Christian faith.

I go up to her to ask where Marie is when she gives me a side hug. "Glad you could make it!" she shouts over the music. She inspects my outfit, and her jaw drops. "You even did your hair! You look amazing!"

"Thank you," I hug her back, my body rigid. I don't usually hug people unless it's my girlfriend or my dad, but it would be rude if I didn't at least hug the host of the party.

"Hey, you made it!" Mason calls to me from behind, holding two plastic cups and handing one to Carrie. He throws his arms around my shoulders. "Dude, I've never seen so many hot chicks in one place. One of them looked like she wanted to stick her tongue down my throat. Life is awesome!"

"Um, what about Harmony?"

"My theory is" – Mason leans in way too close to my face as he talks – "If she sees me with another girl, she'll know I'm irresistible, then jealousy will move her to claim me as hers." He taps his temple with his finger. "It's a brilliant plan."

"Genius," I deadpan. "Where is Marie, anyway?" I turn to ask Carrie.

Carrie grins. I don't know why, but it gives me chills. There's something devious in that head of hers.

She nods toward the stairs. "Just went to the bathroom. Probably to touch up her makeup."

Someone in the distance calls Marie's name. My head whips in that direction in anxious anticipation.

That's when my world turns upside down.

Marie comes down the stairs with a little swagger in her step, revealing a black scoop-neck dress that hangs nicely on her upper body but hugs her curves in the right places. A long pearl necklace wraps gracefully around her neck. Smoky eye makeup makes her green eyes *pop*, and her dark blonde hair is styled in loose curls around her smooth shoulders.

My mouth goes dry, and butterflies take flight in my stomach and flutter up to my chest. The sensation is strong and something I didn't think I was capable of feeling for someone other than Tessa. The living room has shrunk around me, and she's the only person I see. She may as well be wearing a beacon on her forehead. This isn't the adorable skater shoes and ponytail-wearing Marie Burn, I see at school every day.

This is Marie Burn, the sexiest woman I've ever seen in my life.

Marie greets people along the stairwell with hugs and that cheery smile that gets me every time. I can't stop staring. I don't even care that I've been staring.

"Want me to pick your jaw up off the floor?" Carrie says into my ear.

My brain and mouth are disconnected at the moment, so much so that I can't even form a response. I've lost feeling in my legs, and my veins flow with a desire so intense I feel weak in the knees. No one – *no one* – has ever made me feel this way before.

"You're welcome," Carrie says softly into my ear before walking away. I'm too enamored with Marie to address Carrie's cryptic words. I'm deeply grateful for whatever entity turned Marie into an angel sent from heaven.

No, a *goddess*.

Marie finds me and sashays up to me, disrupting my thoughts, heels thumping on the hardwood floor. "Hey! Oh my gosh, you look so good!" she wraps her arms tightly around my torso, making this the first time she has ever hugged me.

Swallowing hard, I slowly snake my arms around her waist. "Thank you," I say, still breathless and trying to understand my current feelings. I pull away so I can give her another once-over. "You look amazing," I tell her. Amazing doesn't even feel like the right word to use in this moment. She's stunning.

"Aw, thanks," she puts her hands on her hips and fixates on me. "You should straighten your hair more often," she takes a strand of my hair and twirls it between her fingers, sending a tingling sensation all over, and it feels so freaking good. That confidence is short-lived, though, when she uneasily combs a strand of hair behind her pearl-studded ears and clears her throat. "Make yourself at home! Drinks are in the kitchen."

Trying to come back to earth, I nod. "Want me to get you anything?"

"Yes, please. Thank you!" she says sweetly, then blinks her eyes wildly, like there's an eyelash stuck in her eye. She's trying to be flirty, but it's not working.

"Is there something in your eye?"

She blushes a ferocious shade of red. "Nope, I'm great," she denies, playing it off. Then she bends over slightly and squeezes her boobs together, giving me a good view of her cleavage. I know Marie has a bubbly, jovial side to her, but I never took her for a flirt. Whatever she's doing right now is different from the Marie I'm used to.

"Okay," I say through pinched vocal cords as she makes her way to the stereo, uncomfortable and defeated. "Um, anything in particular?"

Marie stops and pauses for a second, with her back to me. Then, like a freaking magazine model, she whips her hair flawlessly over her shoulder, fanning out midair and coming together in perfect sync. With a wink, she replies, "Surprise me."

Willing my legs to move, I push through the crowd into the kitchen, with my heart and mind a jumbled mess of emotions that I try to deny and tamper down. There may be a lot of hot girls here, but I'm acutely aware of just one.

Once I fill a second cup with punch, I grab a handful of chips and snack on them, exhaling harshly. I need to get myself together before going back out there. Being at a loss for words and having an out-of-body experience is not something I want to go through in front of Marie the whole night.

"Pop Muzik" by M plays through the speakers, and an explosion of cheers from the crowd erupts throughout the house. Everyone seemed to be looking in the direction of the speakers, where I saw Carrie, Marie, and Mason hanging out.

I grab the two cups and weave through the crowd towards the living room, curious about what got everyone's attention. Maybe someone is doing a handstand, or having a drinking contest, or someone was crazy enough to do the worm on the floor. Either way, I'm intrigued.

Marie dances in the middle of a circle made by the crowd, moving her hips, whipping her hair around, and flinging her arms with a grace that is so unbelievably sexy, but not in a sexual way. Carrie whispers something in her ear while she trains her eyes on me. Marie glances in my direction for a fleeting moment before she eyes the ground and keeps dancing, cheeks flushed and neck sweaty. I lean against the wall and just watch. She's having the time of her life, totally in her element, and it makes me feel things so foreign to me.

The music changes to "Cha Cha Slide" by DJ Casper, and Marie's eyes bug out, and her hands fly up to her cheeks. I go up to her to hand her one of the drinks, then step aside to observe people doing this dance, standing next to Mason. He's totally distracted talking to a hot girl, acting out his "brilliant" plan in front of Harmony, so I'm not going to get much conversation out of him. Though it's entertaining to see how pissed Harmony looks from the other side of the room as she watches Mason flirt.

Marie eyes me and makes a "come hither" gesture with her finger, with a teasing gleam in her eyes. It's hard to say no to a beautiful girl who wants to dance with me.

With resistance nonexistent, I join her with my drink. "Wow, I really didn't have to talk you into dancing," Marie acknowledges.

"What can I say? You're hard to resist," I tell her.

She examines me while she sips from her cup, her squinted eyes not leaving mine. I may have gone too far with that comment, and she knows it. We're just friends, yet I can't refrain from flirting with her with the way she looks tonight.

Marie shakes her hips as the song tells us all to clap, and I stand behind her to copy the steps. This position gives me a fantastic view of her backside. She has a fantastic one. I am a guy, after all.

The song tells us to hop, and we all do so, our drinks sloshing in our cups. "Don't spill your drink," I lean into her ear to warn her, my lips barely grazing the shell of her ear.

"This dance isn't too crazy, I'll be fine," she turns toward me, her lips dangerously close to mine. Eventually, she steps on my foot.

"Crap, I'm sorry," she throws her head back to laugh at herself.

"Are you sure that drink isn't spiked?" I tease.

"Nope, I'm just a klutz."

The music changes to "Vogue" by Madonna, and the whole crowd starts to dance. Marie takes off her shoes, making her a couple of inches shorter, but she's cuter that way. I take off my jacket since it's so hot in here, and I don't miss it when Marie's eyes rake me from head to toe, glossed over with desire.

I grab Marie and twirl her around, moving my hips to the beat. "You're a really good dancer!" she points out.

"I took lessons with my mom growing up. Don't you dare tell anyone," I tell her with a teasing tilt of my lips. She responds by putting her finger to her lips in a *shh* motion.

The events that happen after that are just one wonderful blur. When "Panama" by Van Halen comes on, Marie grips my sleeve as the crowd jumps to the chorus.

Carrie takes photos of everyone with a digital camera and eventually takes a photo of me and Marie with our arms wrapped around each other's waists. I asked Carrie to email me the photos later. Then she squeezes between us and takes a self-portrait photo of the three of us. Mason comes in, and it becomes a four-person self-portrait. I asked Carrie to send me copies of those photos, too.

"I Want You" by Savage Garden plays, and Carrie, Marie, Mason, and I all dance with all our backs facing each other, shaking our hips. Mason makes stupid faces, and our laughing at them brings us to our knees.

"Okay, couples, time to practice for prom," Carrie later says into the microphone and turns on "Holding Back the Years" by Simply Red—a perfect slow dance song.

I'm positive that Marie chose all the songs for tonight, and they were all great songs. My YouTube account is full of songs she's introduced me to now.

"Shall we?" Marie asks in a fancy accent, holding out her hand.

I stare at her outstretched hand, debating with myself. Slow dancing is something couples do, and I've only slow danced with Tessa. It feels wrong to do that with anyone else. As she waits for me to grab her hand, I find my resolve cracking once again.

"Sure," I take her hand in mine, put my other hand on her hip, and sway side-to-side. I may be crossing the line here, but I'm convincing myself to enjoy the moment.

Marie rests her head on my chest and closes her eyes, fully content and peaceful. This, right here, is where I'm supposed to be. The music, the people, none of it exists. It's just me and her, feeling at home together.

"Having fun?" Marie tilts her head to look up at me.

"You know what? I really am," I say, a little shocked. Like Mason, I'm not really a party person, but this has been a great night.

"Well, good, I'm glad," she says in what I believe was supposed to be a Russian accent.

"You did splendidly planning this ball," I counter with my attempt at a British accent.

"Why thank you, Your Majesty," Marie says with an equally bad British accent, dipping her head down to bow to me. I throw my head back and laugh, and she joins me in laughter. Oh, that laugh. Does me in every time.

My eyes land on her big, twinkling, gorgeous ones. So much innocence, sweetness, and heartache rest in those eyes, but paired with her happy, cheerful, funny personality, she's even more remarkable to me.

Before I could stop myself, my hand ran up and down her back in smooth strokes, my fingers leaving a trail of heat in their path. Her eyelids flutter when my other hand cups her cheek. The electricity between us is so intense I can practically taste it.

Slowly, I lean in. Her eyes closed, waiting for me. Then –

"Hold Me Now" by Thompson Twins comes on, and I freeze.

I danced with Tessa to this song. I told her I loved her to this song. Nostalgia hits me in the gut, along with good sense.

What am I doing? I have a girlfriend. A loving, perfect girlfriend that I promised my loyalty to, no matter what happened with us. And here I am, about to kiss someone else that's made my heart do so many flips. Someone who isn't Tessa. Someone who is not, indeed, my girlfriend.

Guilt pulses through me. I shouldn't have come tonight. I shouldn't have danced with Marie the whole time. I should've kept my distance and stayed by Mason's side, even if he was distracted with winning Harmony over.

I need to get out of here.

I don't really want to leave. I really want to see where the night takes us. I want to kiss her. But I can't do that to Tessa.

I can't.

I take Marie's shoulders and push her away. "I'm sorry, I have to go."

"What?" she asks, heartbreak written all over her. God, I'm an awful human.

"I have to go." I step further away from her to grab my jacket by the front door. "I need to just...go. Have a good night, Marie."

Racing down the driveway and down the street, I pull at my hair, tormented and angry with myself. I can't believe I let myself get carried away. I can't believe I almost broke a promise to myself and to Tessa. I can't believe I almost let myself get lost in those shining, plump lips.

Lost in *her*.

I start my car and drive out of the neighborhood in a hurry. During the twenty-minute drive home, I replay the entire night in my mind.

Marie in that sexy dress.

Marie dancing like a backup dancer in a music video.

Marie making me her safe haven when we danced.

Marie laughing and full of joy.

Me, touching her cheek, gazing into her captivating eyes.

What got me the most was that she was ready. She was willing to let me kiss her. She *wanted* me to kiss her. She was okay crossing that line. The only explanation for that is she has feelings for me. And if that's the case, then I'm totally screwed.

What have I done? Where did I go wrong? Why am I struggling so hard with all these emotions, yet I know where my devotion lies?

With urgency, I park my car and run up the steps to my house. It's completely dark inside, which means Dad took this night to hang out with his friends. Which also means I'm going to wallow in self-loathing by myself for the rest of the night.

I don't bother taking my shoes off when I go upstairs to wake up my computer. I hurried to check my email, and I found an unread email from Tessa. *Thank god.* I need to talk to her. I need to know she's still mine. I need her.

Hey sweetie,

I'm glad you made a new friend. Sounds like a sweet girl! And she's a writer, which is a major plus for you, too. Sounds like she would be a good girlfriend for you. You should ask her out! Enjoy the high school experience while you can! – Tessa

A good girlfriend? Ask her out?

I blink. And blink. And blink some more.

"What?" I whisper shout to myself.

This is a stark contrast from our messages in the past. This is someone who has changed from happily in love to total indifference.

I need to get to the bottom of this. Now.

After a few minutes, I've lost count of how many times I read and reread Tessa's email. She seems so ready and willing to let me go. I don't recall agreeing to an open relationship. Tessa didn't want to lose me. If Tessa is as dedicated as I am, she would never recommend that her boyfriend see other people.

Is she...cheating on me?

No, that's insane. She doesn't have a cheating bone in her body. She never even looked at other guys when she was living in Washington. She was terrified of other people except me. We never hung out with other people or other couples, so there's no way that's a possibility. She wouldn't even meet Mason, for god's sake.

Tessa was always afraid. I was the only solid anchor she had in her life. Her parents' presence was few and far between, so I was all she had. Maybe she's afraid I'm already slipping away from her, so letting me go would just be easier for her.

No way am I letting that happen.

A new message from Tessa pops up in my inbox.

I send the email and bury my face in my hands, groaning loudly. The stress of everything is too overwhelming. When I gave Tessa my devotion, I was speaking with the truth with my whole heart. It seemed like honey to her ears when she heard that. I find it hard to believe she would throw that away.

As I sit there in self-loathing, wondering what I'm feeling, Tessa responds to my email.

Everything is wrong with this email. For someone who seemed so worried I would forget about her, she's supportive of me practically cheating on her. She keeps signing off with just her name and doesn't say she loves me. Even if she won't say it, I will. I'm not going anywhere.

The fact that she's worried I would resent her, though, makes sense. That's the only reasonable piece of this email that makes me believe she still loves me.

Dear Tessa,

I would never hold it against you. If anything, I would be glad that I chose you, especially when you come back to Washington. Mr. Nichol is still worried for me, but he should have given up hope months ago. How's Pittsburgh?

Love,

Seth

Leaning back in my chair, I run my hands through my hair and pull. As much as I'm trying to convince Tessa I will choose her, she still seems determined to allow me to be with someone else.

Everything about this feels off.

CHAPTER 10

Marie: Hey! Are you ok?

I close the message. Just as I have the last two times she's sent me an IM. It's been a week since the party. I've avoided Marie at all costs since winter break started. If I'm going to keep my promise to Tessa, I need to distance myself.

"Why aren't you talking to her?" Mason pipes in, popping a pizza roll in his mouth.

"Because I have a girlfriend?" I say like it's the obvious answer.

"That didn't stop you before," he remarks. "Which means only one thing."

"And what would that be, Sigmund Freud?"

"You figured out that you actually have feelings for her, and you're choosing your girlfriend, who is on the other side of the country, rather than go for someone who not only will make you a better person but would also be worth your time."

"Tessa is worth my time," I snap. "My distancing myself from Marie will make it clear to her where I stand."

"Or you could just tell her you need to back off," Mason snaps back. "Better yet, take Tessa up on her offer and move on. God, you're such an idiot."

Right after the name-calling, Mason's cell phone vibrates.

"Hey, pumpkin butt," Mason answers with affection. I turn slowly toward him as he listens on the phone.

Who the crap is pumpkin butt?

"Oh really?" Mason says with seduction. "That would be great. I'll see you in a bit."

"Who's pumpkin butt?" I ask after he hangs up.

"Harmony," he answers casually as he gets up to leave. "Apparently, my technique to make her jealous at the party made her realize she needed this ginger in her life, so she called to meet up at Point Defiance Park."

"You're leaving me to hang out with a girl that's not even your girlfriend?!" I exclaim.

"Consider it payback for all the times you ditched me for your girlfriend. Later, Peaches," Mason practically races out of my room.

"I can't believe Marie told you about her nickname for me!" I shout at him. I can hear him cackle as he runs out of my house.

Giving me a taste of my own medicine. Moron.

Speaking of Tessa, I've been checking my email continuously throughout the break, just hoping to get a message from her. Her responses have been scarce lately, but any time I have a moment to hear from her, it automatically makes my day.

Seth,

Pittsburgh is great! I finally feel like I've settled in. You won't believe this, but I've made some friends here. We hang out and draw during lunch, and they invite me over to their house to watch movies. It's been so fun! I miss you. – Tessa

She's happy and positive. She's made friends. She's goes out in public...willingly. That explains the lack of communication with me. Her emails are still off-putting, though. Something is changing with her, and I can't pinpoint what it is.

I need to play it cool, though.

Dear Tessa,

I'm glad you're happy and settled in. Maybe you can show me the art you've been working on. I've been working on another short story myself.

Love, Seth

So, this is what winter break will be like. Tessa's evasiveness, avoiding Marie and my best friend, ditching me to meet up with his girlfriend.

I never thought my life would come to this.

First day back in school. Marie is sitting next to me in English as usual, but something feels different. Instead of her usual mid-ponytail, her hair is down and curled in loose curls down the shoulders of her gray V-neck shirt. She's improving her game with her appearance, and she looks beautiful.

Even more reason to stay away from her.

The tension is eating me alive. There's an elephant in the room, and it's been there since the party because I refuse to address it. The more I ignore it, the more I feel the elephant will get smaller and eventually turn nonexistent.

At least, I thought I could ignore it until Marie hands me a note.

I have to ask. Do you have feelings for anyone?

Crap.

Crap, crap, crap!

This is the elephant I wanted to leave in the room. Maybe this is a sign that it's time I tell her who owns my heart.

I do like someone. In fact, I'm in love with her.

I pass the note back to her and watch her read it from the corner of my eye. Her expression seems hopeful, even excited in a nervous way.

Can I ask who it is?

If you must know, the angel's name is Tessa. Why?

Marie's face falls into complete devastation. The corners of her lips quiver, and her eyes pool with unshed tears. My answer has deeply hurt her, and there's only one reason why.

My assumption from the beginning was right. She has feelings for me.

Without writing back, she turns toward me and shrugs, not meeting my eyes. "Just curious," she whispers, playing it cool when I know she's far from cool.

With a deep inhale, she crumbles the note and marches to the trashcan close to the door. She slams the paper into it with strong frustration and marches back to her seat. Her face doesn't lie, though, as she hides her face with her hair and avoids eye contact with me. Her heart is broken, and I'm responsible for it.

I'm a terrible person.

When the bell rings, Marie plugs in her headphones and makes a beeline for the door without waiting for me.

"Marie!" I call out to her on my way out of the classroom, but she's already blended with the hoard of students in the hallway. My brain goes into overdrive when I push through to find her, but she's disappeared.

I reach her third-period classroom at the end of the hall and stand at the doorway to look around for Marie but to no avail. Passing period is only five minutes, and I have no plan on what to say, but I didn't want her to spend the third period being hurt. I don't want this to ruin our friendship.

Students are looking in my direction with confused faces, and now I'm making a fool of myself. At a loss, I turn and make my way back down the hall, mind spinning on how to fix this.

During sixth period, I took that opportunity. Marie sits next to me, eyes bloodshot, and makes no effort to peer in my direction. I take out a piece of paper and go back to our old routine of passing notes. I already know the answer, but I want her to feel comfortable talking it out with me, even if it's in writing.

`Tell me the real reason you wanted to know who I liked.`

Marie takes the note and releases a heavy sigh after reading it. The kind of sigh that says she's wiped out emotionally and humiliated that she even brought up this subject.

OKAY, FINE. I LIKE YOU. A LOT. I DON'T KNOW WHAT TO DO ABOUT IT, AND I'M SORRY.

If she's being honest with me, I should be honest with her as well, even though I've spent all my efforts denying it. And this is also where I have to tell her that nothing will ever happen between us.

`Don't be sorry. You feel what you feel. I have to admit, I like you too. You're fun, funny, and really sweet.`

With a brief glance, I see Marie smile sadly as she writes a response.

THANK YOU. UNFORTUNATELY, THAT DOESN'T MAKE ME FEEL BETTER.

`I'm really sorry. I never wanted to hurt you. But I really do like you.`

YOU'RE JUST SAYING THAT TO MAKE ME FEEL BETTER.

`No, I really do. It's just...I'm in love with someone else.`

DOES SHE GO TO THIS SCHOOL?

`No, she moved to Pittsburgh a couple of months ago.`

It's very faint, but I hear Marie scoff derisively. My immediate feeling is to be offended by her judgmental attitude, but she's hurting, and I still want to make this better. She knows where I stand, and she can move on to someone else.

I retrieve the note from her and write down what I really hope she will agree to. Even though I thought my distance over winter break was something I had to do, I realized I couldn't do that permanently. She's made my life better, and I can't lose that.

`I would still love to be friends, though.`

Marie stares at the note with anger in her eyes, which I don't understand why. I'm not even cutting her off. I still want her in my life if she'll have me.

I THINK I CAN DO THAT.

`Good, I'm glad. Does this mean I'm still allowed in your convertible?` ☺

LOL, I SUPPOSE SO ☺

The bell rings, and I pack up my stuff, but Marie exits the classroom without waiting for me, making that the second time today she's done that. I watch her go, mentally exhausted from the events of today.

And she took our notes with her.

"Hi, this is Tessa. Leave a message, and I'll call you back. If I feel like it," Tessa ends her voicemail with a giggle.

The last email I sent her was almost a week ago, asking her to send me any new artwork she's doing. She mentioned drawing with some new friends; I want to see what she's doing. She's either not near her phone or she puts me through to her voicemail.

This was the third time I've tried calling her this week, making this the third time I've gotten her voicemail. Instead of overwhelming her with new IMs or missed calls, I decided to wait for her to reach out to me when she had time. While I wait, impatience eats me alive.

Then there's Marie. Since she admitted her feelings, things have mended back to the way they used to be. The only change is that Mason and I hang out with her and Carrie at the second-floor stage every morning before the first bell. Harmony has begun to join us, too, since she and Mason are officially the new nerdy couple. With her long brown hair, thick-rimmed glasses, quiet disposition, and face void of any makeup, she's the perfect nerdy match for Mason. Mostly we play card games like BS (which Carrie insists stands for Blake Shelton because, according to Marie, she's obsessed with hot men) and Egyptian Rat Screw, which made me chuckle every time someone said it. It's actually called Egyptian War, yet there's an even weirder name attached to it.

Just like she did at the party, Carrie brought her camera with her and took pictures of us playing games. "It's our senior year; we may never do this again," she said. We go with the flow and take all the pictures Carrie desires.

Marie and I have more classes together this semester than we did last semester. I didn't expect that to happen, so I suppose I could have kept our relationship strictly at school instead of giving her my phone number before winter break. It wasn't going to be enough, though. I wanted more. At a friendly level, of course.

Thoughts of Tessa invade my mind while I write about a story taking place in a forest, and then I randomly get an IM from her.

Tessa: I'm so sorry I've been missing your calls, babe. I've been busy with Tamara and Celeste. They've been helping me finish my comic. They've helped me a lot since I moved here! Plus, my parents have been cracking down on me graduating this year. I've been so tired when I get home that I just plop in bed. Tell me what's new in your life!

I reply to Tessa and tell her that I've started writing a story that takes place in a forest. I sent the message, only to find that Tessa had gone offline a moment ago. It seems our relationship has taken a backseat in her life.

Frustration clouds my vision. Either she's been busy with her new friends, or her parents are watching her like hawks. That part wouldn't make sense, though. Her parents didn't care what she did when she lived in Federal Way, so something tells me she's not telling the truth. She may be remorseful, but she's not doing anything to make time for me. We're pulling apart, and I'm scared of what is to come if this continues.

Those are the thoughts that kept me awake that night, so much so that I got on my Instant Messenger to see who's online to talk to about it.

I'm surprised to see Marie still logged in. It's nine o'clock, and she's not in bed yet. Nonetheless, I want to talk to her. Marie is my friend, and she knows that I'm devoted to Tessa, so I should be able to talk about this with her. She should be understanding enough to give impartial advice.

Seth: *I can't sleep.*

It's about a minute or so before she responds, which brings a wave of relief.

Marie: *Why? What's wrong?*

A smile spreads on my face. I knew she would respond. She's one of the kindest, most compassionate people I know.

Seth: *I miss Tessa. But I'm scared she doesn't miss me. She doesn't tell me she loves me anymore. I'm scared I'm losing her. But I want to stick it out because I told her I would. And I don't want to just up and leave like my mom did, as you know.*

Marie: *I understand.*

I thought she would offer more context, and there's nothing indicating that she's typing more. So, I offer the biggest confession I have so far.

Seth: *She's even been trying to get me to date you.*

Marie: *Really?*

Seth: *Yeah. She doesn't want me to miss out on the high school experience. If she hadn't moved, she probably wouldn't even suggest it.*

Seth: *God, I wish she never moved. I miss her like crazy.*

Immediately, I feel better getting this off my chest. Every minute that passes, though, Marie doesn't respond. My messages become word vomit after that. I confess everything I've been doing in my time alone.

Seth: *Sometimes, at night, I hold my own hand just to pretend she's still with me.*

Seth: *I even hold a pillow to pretend I'm holding her.*

Marie still doesn't offer a response. I assume she's writing or getting ready for bed, or her mom wanted to talk to her. She's told me her mom likes to come in with a glass of wine and chat about random stuff. I started to miss my own mom. That is until I remember that I'm mad at her for deciding to run off with another woman, dropping us like flies.

Marie: *I gotta go.*

Before I can respond, Marie goes offline. I freeze and stare at the screen, trying to understand her abrupt departure. What made her cut off the conversation like that? Did I offend her somehow?

No. That can't be right. I didn't say anything to hurt her feelings. Hardly anything offends her anyway.

"You okay?" I ask Marie when I follow her into the school the next morning.

Marie's eyes are bloodshot, and dark circles are present under them. Worry spikes within me seeing her so depressed. Marie deserves all the happiness in the world, yet she looks like she's been crying for hours.

"Yeah, I'm okay," she replies with a ghost of a smile. Her smile and happy disposition are absent, replaced with a frown and a blank expression. I don't believe what she's saying, and now I'm even more worried.

"Didn't sleep good?"

"Yeah," she says plainly.

"Is your mom okay?" I press. I should stop prying, but I just want her to be happy.

"She's fine," she states curtly. She clearly isn't telling me something. She seemed fine up until she cut off our conversation last night, but I don't know what exactly I said to make her so upset.

As we ascend the stairs to the second-floor stage, Marie remains quiet, and I'm uncomfortable. I don't know what else to do, so I stay silent, too.

When we reach the stage, Carrie is there waiting like usual, along with Mason and Harmony, who are cuddling on the stage away from Carrie. Carrie's usually pleasant disposition is missing when she glares at me. Not just an ordinary, dirty look, but she has pure fury and hatred that could cut me to pieces.

What did I do?

Carrie's eyes then meet Marie's, and her expression softens, but only a little, with a lot of reluctance behind it.

Moving past the awkwardness, I hold my hand out to Marie for an earbud. She hesitates, but her lips quirk to the side, and she hands me one. We listen to "In the Groove" by Kim Waters, and our vibe is completely off balance the whole time. I convince myself it will get better. By the time I saw her in English class, her disposition seemed to have improved from earlier this morning.

Mrs. Buhler claps as a signal to start the class. "Okay, we're well into the second semester, and it's to talk about" – she pauses when she turns on the projector, showing us a T-chart that reflects on the whiteboard – "your final project!"

Everyone in the class groans, including me. If I did this final, it would help me graduate high school, which involves me putting in the work. That doesn't appeal to me, but not because of my attitude towards education.

Today is Valentine's Day. My valentine isn't with me to celebrate this day, and I'm in a sour mood because of it. The only thing I might be able to do is send Tessa flowers or chocolates, but I don't have the money to do that. There's no way Dad would give me the money to do it anyway, considering his lack of support for this relationship. Things are already rocky as it is. On a day that's all about love, I'm at a loss. It infuriates me.

"Oh, relax," Mrs. Buhler waves her hand dismissively, enhancing my already crappy mood. "I'm telling you now, so you have a few months to work on it. Now" – she addresses the class – "As you can see, one side of this chart here is a list of plays by famous playwrights, and the other side is a list of human traits. What you'll be doing is picking a play and then matching it with a human trait that best fits the overall theme of the play. For example, for Hamlet, you might pick revenge. For Julius Caesar, you might pick betrayal, or power-hungry, and so on." She points at us when she says, "Your job for this final is to tell me how this trait is shown in the play and how that trait is still prevalent today."

Marie writes vigorously on a piece of paper like the diligent student she is. I cross my arms and glance at my feet, impatiently waiting for class to end. If I was more interested, this might be a cool final to work on.

"Any questions?" Mrs. Buhler's eyes search the room.

A punk kid in a sock hat raises his hand and asks, "Do we have to present this in front of the class?"

"Well, of course," she answers with such positivity I could vomit.

The whole class groans even louder. Some even exclaim, "Aw, come on, man!" and hang their heads. Marie blows a huge breath and rests her chin on her hand. Yeah, she's not looking forward to it either, even though she's a hard worker when it comes to school.

Mrs. Buhler's phone rings at her desk right after she tells us when the final is due, which happens to be a few days before graduation.

"Think about what you want to do for your final while I take this," she tells us when she rounds her desk to answer the phone.

Students start whispering to each other, and I can hear Mason ask Marie, "What are you doing for the final?"

With a sly smile, she answers, "That's for me to know and for you to find out."

"Ouch!" Mason folds his arms in a playful pout.

"Marie, they want you at the front office," Mrs. Buhler tells Marie when she hangs up her office phone, which snaps me into focus. Marie never gets called to the front office.

Lips turned down in confusion, Marie shrugs, not knowing what this is about either. She gets up from her seat to grab a hall pass from Mrs. Buhler and leaves the classroom. I snort disdainfully when the class "oohs" like she's done something bad. Mrs. Buhler talks further about the final as I pull out my notebook to doodle.

A few minutes go by, and Marie comes back into the classroom with a blush...and holding a bouquet of flowers close to her chest.

My eyes lock in on the roses and carnations. A bouquet of flowers? Who had the audacity to send her flowers?

Sure, Marie is a gorgeous girl, and she knows Tessa is my girlfriend, but someone is showing enough interest in her to send her flowers. I can't think of anyone I've seen her talk to who would be showing interest in her like this.

This doesn't sit well with me. At all.

Marie sits down at her desk with the flowers while the whole class "oohs and "ahs" over her, this time in adoration. I make sure not to acknowledge her presence as I pretend to write in my notebook.

"Who got you flowers?" Mason whispers to Marie.

"I don't know," she whispers back. "It just says 'secret admirer.'"

I swallow down the growl of anger in my throat that begs me to come out. This guy, whoever he is, is playing it slick. Using "secret admirer" as a way to get her hooked first and sending her flowers to win her heart. Fury boils in the pit of my stomach at the thought of her being with some guy.

After class, Marie and I walked to her next class together, as usual. The only difference here is that I'm not talking. Instead, I'm stewing in my negative emotions. Marie may or may not be talking. I don't know, and I don't really care. I stare straight ahead, glaring at everything and everyone.

"What are you doing for the final? Or are you not going to do it at all?" Marie's sweet voice, followed by her giggle, breaks my concentration when we reach her classroom. I was so deep in thought I didn't realize we reached her classroom. I shake my head and turn to reply. Examining her grinning at me, my frustration fades, and I forget why I was so mad –

Until I look down at the flowers she's holding up to her chest.

Now I'm mad all over again.

"Why don't you ask your 'secret admirer'?" I sneer, using air quotes. Before she can reply with a comeback, I spin at my heel and ditch her. Her eyebrows squint in question as the distance grows between us.

You're such a jerk, Harris.

At lunch, I stare daggers in Marie's direction as she giggles with Carrie and waves the flowers around. My eyes are more in the direction of the flowers than at her, but I'm still angry.

"I don't get why you're so pissed off," Mason says as he stuffs his mouth with a chicken sandwich.

His statement ruminates in my mind. I love Tessa. There's no doubt in my mind about that. I told Marie that myself. I also told her I liked her while also making it clear nothing would ever happen between us. At this moment, though, I want to be the only guy Marie sees. I want to be the only guy that gives her attention. Yet I can't stop the look of murder in my face as she talks with Carrie during lunch with those stupid flowers lying next to her on the table. She's blushing and giggling happily, and that makes me angrier.

She *likes* the attention this person is showing her.

"You're not this grumpy when any other girl gets flowers," Mason adds.

"What's there to be grumpy about?" I grumble, stuffing a fry in my mouth. "She's happy. I'm happy she's getting attention from someone." The words feel like acid on my tongue.

"You're so full of crap." Mason grins like a moron, then points at me. "You're acting like a jealous boyfriend, yet you don't want to date her."

I have no good response on hand, so I shrug. "Whatever. It's fine."

Mason smacks me upside the head, his countenance suddenly annoyed. "Cut the crap!" he snaps as I whip my head back in shock. "You're jealous, but you refuse to admit it. You like her, but you don't want to like her. Yet you're determined to stay with Tessa. Face it, man. You need to figure out who it is you want."

Whether I have a right to feel this way or not is not the point. She's getting attention from someone that isn't me. That's all there is to it. I don't have to like it. To any logical person, my reasoning would make no sense.

"I want Tessa," I said pointedly. "I love her. Marie knows that."

Mason eyes me skeptically and shakes his head. "I smell drama."

I continue to view Marie from afar, who's getting up to leave her table with Carrie and grabbing her flowers with her. I chose Tessa, and that decision won't change. That was the best thing I could do. I'm keeping my promise, whether my heart wants to or not.

"You've been acting kind of weird today," Marie brings out as we cross the courtyard after school with those god-forsaken flowers. "Are you okay?"

No. Someone else is noticing you, and I don't want him to. I want to be the only thing you see.

Obviously, I can't tell her that, even though my insides beg me to snatch the bouquet out of her hands and stomp on them. "Yeah, I'm fine. Sorry." Keep it brief, and let it be. That's how I'm going to roll here.

"You didn't send me these flowers, did you?" she motions toward the bouquet in her hands, full of hope.

"No," I answer through my teeth. I was doing just fine, not talking about those stupid things the rest of the day, but here we are, talking about it and rubbing it in my face. I grind my molars together to keep from saying something I'll regret.

"So weird," she says more to herself than to me. "I can't think of anyone who would have sent these."

A sigh escapes my lips. "Neither can I."

"I really want to know who my secret admirer is. Oh well," she shrugs and hands me a headphone, which she struggles to do while carrying the flowers. "What do you want to listen to?"

"Not in the mood." I walk toward the parking garage, ditching her once again, making a fool of myself. I'm too into my own head to act like everything is fine.

CHAPTER 11

Tessa: Hey Seth, I'm so sorry I keep missing your calls and messages. Tell me how you're doing.

Lately, this has been the norm. I call her, and leave a message, and she will only message me through IM to apologize for missing my calls. Now, she doesn't even explain what she's been doing; she just expects me to understand while she lives her life. She doesn't even have a pet name for me anymore. Sending me a message seems like a chore for her now, just to keep me satisfied.

This just pisses me off. So much so that I closed her message; she won't care if I respond anyway. Clearly, I don't mean as much to her as she does to me. I would talk this out with her, but it's complicated when she won't return my calls.

Marie's logged in. I'll just talk to her about it. Mason is logged in also, but I already know what he will say on the matter.

Seth: Hey. Can you talk?

Marie: Yeah. Are you ok?

How do I answer this question? Honestly, I'm all over the place. I'm emotionally and mentally exhausted from what has become a one-sided relationship. Nonetheless, a promise is a promise.

Marie hasn't gotten any more flowers from her "secret admirer" since Valentine's Day, but it brought me a rude awakening. For months, I loved that she had eyes for me. I loved that we were such close friends while she had a crush on me. The moment she got those flowers, I realized that someone else might be fighting for her attention but too shy to come out and say it. It rubs me the wrong way.

Seth*: Just mad that my relationship with Tessa isn't the way it should be. I'm always trying to call her. And, of course, she doesn't call me back.*

Marie*: I'm sorry.*

I wait for her to type more, but she doesn't. Is that all she's going to say? As a friend, I thought she would show more support. Maybe offer some sort of encouragement that Tessa still loves me.

Seth*: Thanks.*

She doesn't offer anything else, but she doesn't log out either. If this conversation were happening in person, there would be awkward silence. I feel a sense of disappointment that the conversation has seemingly ended when I really wanted to keep talking about Tessa. I also don't want to stop talking to Marie.

As I stare at the screen, thinking of something to say, my cell phone vibrates. "Mom" shows up on the front screen, and I groan. I should just block her. Not just on my phone but on my Instant Messenger as well. I thought after months of failing to get a hold of me, it would make her stop trying, but Debra Harris fights for what she wants. Marie has told me more than once to give her a chance; I can't bring myself to do it.

I put Mom through to voicemail once again and face the glowing screen in front of me. The stress of my strained relationship has taken a toll on me. The stress has invaded my life, and I'm starting to feel the way I did when my parents divorced. More than anything, I want to go back to the moment when I was truly happy, where everything felt normal.

Then Marie surprises me with another message.

Marie*: Sounds like you need to get out and have some fun.*

Odd. She happened to say the very thing I was thinking about. Marie is a fun, carefree person. She would be the perfect person to do something to take me away from my troubles.

__Seth__: Any ideas?
__Marie__: I have one...
__Seth__: Care to tell me?
__Marie__: Nope ☺
__Seth__: Oh, come on, Katharine Hepburn!
__Marie__: Just you wait, Peaches. It's gonna be fun.

Beep beep.

The sound of a car horn wakes me out of a deep sleep, and my "grouchy" switch turns on. It's Saturday morning. No one should be honking this early on a weekend.

Beep beep.

For the love of god.

I turn over in my bed and put the pillow over my head, hoping to drown out the obnoxious noise and the bright sun peeking through my curtains. It's too early for this crap.

My hopes diminish when I hear the vibrating of my phone on my nightstand. Someone is determined to interrupt my sleep, and it's annoying as all get out.

I lazily slap my hand around my nightstand to grab my phone. It falls to the floor in a loud thud that spikes my irritation. Finally, I blindly find my phone and flip it open.

"Hello?" I answer grouchily without looking at the caller ID.

"Well, aren't you just chipper!" I hear a girly voice say cheerfully.

I recognize that voice, and it's not Tessa. "Marie?"

"Yes, sir. Hello," she announces with an unidentifiable accent. As annoyed as I was initially, that gets a chuckle out of me. "How's it going?"

"It's Saturday morning," I grumble.

"It's noon, Peaches," she points out. "Now come downstairs; I have a surprise for you."

The line goes dead before I can say no. Curiosity on how she found out where I lived is the prime motivator that gets me out of bed. I slip on my Converse without tying the laces and throw my flannel pajama pants on. As I pad across the front lawn, I see Marie parked at the curb in her baby blue Mazda Miata, sunglasses on, hair straight and windblown, playing with the radio.

I'm not going to deny it anymore. I've tried to for months now, and I fail every time. The harder I try, the more exhausting it gets. As of now, no more denial and no more fighting my feelings.

Marie Burn is downright hot.

"Hey, sleepyhead," she coos at me with a sly grin.

"What's happening right now?" I ask groggily, eyeing the car from hood to trunk and admiring the beige leather interior.

Marie exudes confidence when she says, "Well, I know you need to get out and have some fun," she rests her arm on top of the steering wheel and twists her body toward me. "And I also remember you telling me how you missed riding in a convertible, so I thought I'd keep my word and take you for a ride." She puts on a poorly done gangster accent when she says, "Why? Do I look like I'm delivering Chinese food or something?"

My body stays rooted in place, stunned. It was at least six months ago that I told her about that treasured memory of mine. I can't believe she remembered that, and I mainly told her about it in passing.

"This is so weird. How? Wha-?" My head can't seem to formulate the right questions to ask as my gaze switches from her to the sidewalk and back to my house. "How do you even know where I live?"

"First off –" she lifts a finger in protest, "This is not weird. I promised you a surprise, and here I am. Second, Mason gave me your address when I blackmailed him that I would tell Harmony that he sleeps with a Transformer robot. Now hurry up and put on clothes that are not pajamas."

"You're crazy, you know that?" I tell her with mirth in my tone, hands on my hips.

"Oh, I know I'm crazy," she acknowledges with no shame. "And I know you've got some crazy in you too." She taps the side of her head. "I can sense it. The question is, who the crap cares?"

I tilt my head back and put on a thinking face, even though I had already made up my mind.

"I'll get changed."

I sprint across my front lawn and race up the stairs, my mind whirling with the events of this morning. Any other person might be weirded out by this, but this is a pleasant surprise for me. I only have one friend, and he doesn't show up at my house like this for the fun of it.

Once I get into a baggy pair of jeans with my gray jacket and white t-shirt, I strut back towards her car. "Where are we going?"

"Don't worry about it." She smirks as she gets out of the car. "Want to drive us to the freeway? If I let you go any further, Mom would kill me."

My jaw drops while I tamper down my jittered nerves. "Are you serious?"

She shrugs. "Why not? You've always wanted to drive one. Now's your chance. Hop in, Peaches."

I dash to the other side of the car and get in the driver's seat, my mind currently blown. Ten minutes ago, I was annoyed that someone was calling me on a Saturday morning, and now I'm about to fulfill one of my long-lived dreams. A dream that would have stayed on my wish list if Marie never waltzed into my life.

"Oh crap," I mutter to myself, seeing the stick shift in front of me.

"You don't know how to drive a manual, do you?" Marie cringes.

Slightly embarrassed, I shake my head, my hand lying on the clutch.

"That's okay," she reassures me. "I'll teach you. Let's just go from here to the end of the street. Once you get comfortable, then we can go further."

I blow out an uneasy breath. "I don't want to wreck your car."

"You won't," Marie pats my shoulder. "Okay, with your left foot, push down the clutch pedal and shift to first gear."

I do as she says and drive at a snail's pace down the street. Once I have my bearings, I shift into second, then third. Marie teaches me how to stop, then encourages me to go faster once we reach downtown. I kill the engine a couple of times, but Marie shows patience when she tells me to try again.

"When you're stopped on a hill, and you have to move," she coaches me. "You have to balance the clutch pedal with the gas so you don't kill the engine. We're kind of close to a small hill, so give it a try."

Tacoma has hills all over the place. Some are extremely steep, especially the ones that are close to our school. Some hills are just long. Getting this skill down might take a little longer. Shifting into first, I gradually lift my foot off the clutch, then press the gas lightly. We begin to roll backward until I press the gas harder. The car shakes a bit, then dies.

"For crying out loud," I grumble.

"It's okay! You're doing really good!" Marie cheers me on when I get the car started again. "Let's just get back on the main road, and we can head to the freeway."

I drive us through downtown Tacoma, crossing over railroad tracks and old historic buildings, taking in the scenery. Marie's hair flows behind her in a liquid gold waterfall, her small fingers combing through the strands to get it out of her face. I force myself to keep my eyes on the road; otherwise, staring at the beauty next to me will get us in trouble.

"Let's get a picture to commemorate this moment," Marie pipes in.

I manage to pull us over successfully on a flat area when she pulls out a disposable Kodak camera. She leans in close to me while positioning the camera correctly. As her hair whips in my direction, I'm intoxicated with her fruity and sugary sweet aroma. It fits Marie perfectly.

I inch my head closer to hers while she clicks the camera multiple times. "All right, I'm satisfied. I'll take us on the freeway from here."

We switch spots, and before I know it, we're cruising the freeway up towards Seattle, wind blowing through our hair. Marie plays "There She Goes" by The La's through the stereo, singing along and raking her hand through her dark blonde hair.

In the last six months, Marie has helped me write better, expanded my taste in music, given me useful advice on improving my life (although I haven't put it into practice), taught me card games, and now she's helping me learn to drive a stick shift. Never did I think I would be at this point in my life. Trying new things and learning along the way. I don't know how I lived this long without her.

"How do you not have sunglasses?" she shrieks, which makes me realize I have been gawking at her much longer than is appropriate.

"I hardly wear them," I shrug.

"Well, there's a few pairs of sunglasses in there if the sun is blinding you." She points at the glove box in front of me.

I lift the handle of the glove box, and a waterfall of sunglasses pours out of it. "Holy crap, why do you have so many?" I inquire, fishing through the sea of sunglasses that have landed on the floor of my seat.

"Friends leave them in there, and I just don't say anything," she says with humor in her tone.

I pick up the biggest pair I can find and slide them on my nose. "So you're a thief?"

"Not if they don't say anything!" Marie laughs, then she keeps singing to the song. "'There she goes; there she goes again, chasing down my lane...'"

Her singing sucks me in. As I resume gawking at her once more, I examine everything about her: her full lips curved in a happy smile, soft hair that makes me want to reach out and touch it, smooth white skin, and her short stature leaning up very closely toward the steering wheel so her tiny feet can reach the gas pedal.

The way I felt about her at the party came screaming back with fierce intensity. With no more shame in me, I welcome it. She's the most charming and adorable girl I've ever known. Inside and out.

Marie does a double take from the road to my face with huge sunglasses. "You look like a demented dragonfly."

"Can a dragonfly even be demented?"

"Apparently, yes, because you look like one."

"Pick up the Pieces" by Kenny G starts to play. My head involuntarily starts bobbing to the upbeat saxophone notes, and Marie dances in her seat, shimmying her shoulders. Watching her dance is no hardship from where I'm sitting, even if her moves are dorky.

"You like this song?" she asks me.

Surprising myself, I nod. "It's catchy."

"Aw, I've rubbed off on you! You like jazz music," she says in a singsong voice, prodding my arm.

"It's okay." I attempt to put on a nonchalant attitude, but I fail every time my body moves to the music.

"No, don't you deny it, Peaches," she good-humoredly wiggles her finger in my face. "You like it."

I tilt my head from one shoulder to the other, pretending to debate her argument. "Okay, Katharine Hepburn, you win."

"Ha! I knew it!" she belts out. "Now, let's take this up a notch."

Marie shifts to fifth gear, and we speed up past the legal limit. I hold onto the door as the force of speed pushes me against the back of the seat. A laugh escapes me as we wind the freeway toward Federal Way, loving the rush of adrenaline. "Words" by Missing Persons starts to play, and Marie starts dancing again.

"Yeah, that's what I'm talking about!" she shoots her arm in the air and cheers. I cheer along with her, leaning back in my seat as much as possible, raising my arms in the air and letting the sun warm my face.

This is what pure bliss feels like. It's liberating to be away from the constant negativity in my life and the constant reminder of my heart being divided in two. I get tired of it all, and reliving the best memory of my life is taking that all away.

Marie is my saving grace.

"Want some Tully's?" Marie asks once she takes the next exit after passing Federal Way.

"Sure!"

"Bittersweet Symphony" by The Verve starts playing, its boosting melody softly filling the air around us. It's the kind of song that could instill encouragement and hope in someone.

"Oh! I love this song," Marie says in a wistful manner, her mouth curved into a melancholy smile.

As we keep driving, I can't help but notice Marie's silence, and her features, which were once lighthearted and gleeful, have turned downcast, trying not to cry. The song has the ability to tug at heartstrings with its emotional and somewhat romantic melody.

She sighs audibly when the song trails off, and it goes silent between us. "Kind of depressing," she chuckles nervously.

I have a feeling there's more to that statement than she's letting on.

Once we get to Tully's, Marie orders a large cinnamon roll for us to share that I offered to pay for. Sharing this pastry with a remarkable girl, like a cute couple, feels so intimate. It should feel wrong, but it doesn't. It feels great.

It feels *right*.

We take our delectable pastry to the rustic loft upstairs and go to town in its sugary warmth. "Thith thinamon woll ith tho ooey," I comment with my mouth full.

"I know! Ish sho shexy," Marie replies with her mouth full as well.

I nearly spit out my food in laughter, so much so that I have to cover my mouth and regain my composure enough to swallow. "Did you just call that sexy?"

"Yes, yes I did," she confirms, stabbing her fork into the roll and tearing off another bite.

"I've never heard of food being described as sexy."

"Now you have."

We both laugh and finish off the roll, and Marie sips from her hot chocolate. I study her expression as the light from the window covers her face and illuminates her eyes, making them brighter. Now is as good a time as any to bring up what has been nagging me since the car ride.

"So," I say while I clear my throat. "You seemed kind of depressed when you played that one song."

"What song?" She eyes me inquisitively.

"The one where he says 'bittersweet symphony.'"

That gets a smirk out of her. "You mean the song called Bittersweet Symphony?"

"Yeah, that one."

She avoids eye contact and peers out the window again. "My ex broke up with me before the beginning of the school year," she begins. "He didn't want to be tied down when he was in college. Free to do whatever he wanted. And as I would cry in my room over a guy who was dumber than a rock, I listened to that song. The music itself is emotional, but the lyrics got to me. When he says 'I can't change my mold', I realized I needed to be happy with who I am, and not let some guy change me. Then he says 'I feel free now', and I realized I felt the same way." She sips from her dark green Tully's cup and sighs. "It may not make sense, and it might not be what the song is about, but that's how I took it."

I stare at her in wonder. She reaffirmed everything I thought the first time we went to Tully's together. Marie is stronger than she gives herself credit for. She makes a good point. Her ex really is dumber than a rock. She was disposable to him.

You are so far from disposable, Marie.

"So that's kind of what helped me through it," Marie adds.

Grinding my molars, I take a deep breath to get myself together to stop myself from flipping the table in anger. God, that guy was such a douchebag. I wish I could grab her and kiss her just to let her know how much she means to me. That someone appreciates and cares for her. That I'm the one who can show her that. Not the one trying to win her heart with flowers, whoever he is. No one found out who that guy was.

"I'm sorry," I say sincerely. "If it helps at all" – I pause before I tell her what I really think of her – "you're amazing, Marie."

Marie blushes hard and hides her face behind her cup. "Thank you," she says, then adds shyly, "You're amazing, too. Even if you don't think so."

Hiding my shy smile, I slap my cheeks to hide the heat building in them.

"Look at that, I made Seth Harris blush." Marie points at me and giggles.

"Stop it," I say with my best feminine voice and wave my hand, making Marie laugh harder.

We finish our drinks and make our way out of the coffee shop. I watch Marie as we go back to her Miata parked at the curb, examining how her jeans hug her perfect backside, her V-neck shirt clings in the right places, and her hair straightened and reaches the middle of her back. In the past, all of this – checking her out, hanging out with her, talking on the phone – would have made me guilt-ridden, and I would have talked myself into saying we're just friends and my loyalty still rests with Tessa.

None of that has crossed my mind.

I can't get in the car with Marie again. I need to talk to Tessa. I need to know she's still my girl. I need to take some time alone and clear my head. My head and heart are not on the same page, and I need to figure out an action plan.

"Actually, Marie, I think I'm going to walk home," I say, pointing my thumb behind me. "It's a nice day, and I don't live that far away."

"Are you sure?" she replies with concern.

"I'll be fine. But I had a blast today. Thank you for showing me how to have fun again."

She looks up at me and shows off the smile that makes me hold my breath. "It was great. I'm just glad you don't plan on getting a restraining order against me...right?"

I break our gaze. "No, you're safe."

Hands in my pockets, I stand there awkwardly. My mind is screaming at me to leave. Turn around, walk away, and don't look back. My heart is telling me another story. It wants me to stay. My feet won't move. I want to keep being with her. The girl who has brought a bright light into the darkness of my life. The girl that's been through so much but still shines the brightness of the sun. The girl who knows how to have fun and carry a conversation. The girl who asks if I'm okay when I'm down. The girl who gave me her last Snickers bar to make me feel better.

My self-control is snapping. I can feel it.

I take a couple of strands of her hair and softly comb them behind her ear. Marie closes her eyes and licks her lips, inviting mine to touch hers. The lips I want to kiss so badly.

Her breathing quickens, watching me with inquiring eyes, but she doesn't move to stop me. My hands slowly move down the sides of her neck and land on her shoulders, where I grip them and slowly inch myself toward her, repeating what happened at the party. What I almost did. What I'm about to do.

My heart is racing. The electric pull between us is stronger than anything I've ever felt. So strong, that it begs me to explore it. See where it takes us. The expectation of what is to come, blended with the nerves pulsing through me, brings me back to my first kiss with Tessa.

Tessa.

I have a girlfriend.

I made a promise.

What am I doing? This is the second time since I've met her that I've been tempted to kiss her.

Before my lips move any closer, I take a step back. Marie's eyes turn hurt and devastated, just like they did at the party.

"I'm sorry, I shouldn't..." I shake my head. Guilt, my old friend, rushes back to remind me of how stupid I'm being and it consumes me. I turn and walk away down the sidewalk, away from her. The one thing I didn't want to do again, and here I am doing just that. My brain nags me with second guesses, causing me to wonder if I made the right choice.

Don't look back. Don't look back. Keep walking.

Ignoring my self-conflict, I turn around. Marie has gone back to her car, head hung low and dejected. Why does it feel awful to do the right thing?

That chemistry, though. My first kiss with Tessa didn't come close to what I had felt when I was about to kiss Marie. The butterflies didn't just take flight in my stomach. They took flight in my entire body, weakening my knees and clouding my senses. It felt...wonderful. Mesmerizing. All of it felt so right.

I want to feel that again. I want to feel her lips against mine. Marie makes me feel alive. I don't want that ever to go away.

Forcing my feet to move, I run back to Marie before she gets back into her car. Her eyes brighten up the moment she sees me, wondering what exactly I'm doing. I'm wondering the same thing, but I will punish myself later.

At last, after all these months, I give in to temptation when I take her face in my hands and kiss her hard. A whimper escapes her, and she shuts her eyes tightly. My eyes involuntarily close, and I let myself feel everything: the sensation of her lips, the butterflies that make me weak, how good she feels in my arms, being close to her, her scent of fruit and sweetness that reflects everything she is.

Marie stays rigid for a moment until her hands slide around my waist and pulls me closer. She opens for me, our lips moving in perfect tandem. Her kisses are desperate and needy, just as I was feeling for her. I hold her face tighter, and she grips me tighter. I can't breathe. I can't get enough of her. I want more.

So much more.

After making out in the street for a while, I pull away and gaze into her eyes. They're clouded in a mixture of pure joy and pleasure. My mind is still muddled from how mind-blowing that was, and my heart screams for more. More so than it ever has for a kiss.

What have I done?

I broke my promise.

"I'm sorry, Marie," I say, voice shaky. "That shouldn't have happened."

Remorse consuming every fiber of my being, I turn on my heel and walk down the sidewalk. I made a huge mistake. I did the one thing I vowed I would never do.

I turned into my mother.

I rake my hands through my unkempt hair and pull on it until it hurts. I welcome the pain. I deserve all the bad things that happen to me from here on out. I deserve all the hate and anger Tessa will no doubt spew my way when I tell her what I did. Mason will no doubt have a word with me, and this time, I won't fight back. Marie will never talk to me again when I have to push her away once more. I'm ready to accept all the consequences of my actions.

A girly shout in the distance causes me to turn to the source. Marie is next to her car, arms in the air and spinning in circles in the street.

"HE KISSED ME!" she screams to the sky. "HE KISSED ME! LET THE WORLD KNOW HE KISSED ME!"

The honking of a car horn interrupts her cheering. She rights herself and shuffles to her car. The blunder of emotions flowing through me prevents me from laughing at her overflowing bliss. I can't bring myself to be as delighted as she is.

I know what I have to do, and it's going to be excruciating.

CHAPTER 12

Marie has been trying to talk to me all day. Yet I'm doing everything I can to avoid her.

I spent the rest of the weekend figuring out how I could keep my distance but not lose Marie completely, all the while maintaining a relationship with Tessa. I came up with nothing. I made a mess, and I need to clean it up. Until I figure out what to do and I'm ready to tell Marie, I'm staying far away from her. No morning hangouts, no going to class together, none of that.

Even during lunch, I avoid her. On the brick garden where I used to hang out in the mornings, I lay along the edge on my back, deep in thought, with my arm draped over my eyes. I never go outside during lunch, but I know Marie sits close to where I usually eat.

I hear the thud of a backpack close to me. Then I feel someone grab my knee and wiggle it. I move my arm and see Marie sitting next to my feet. Just when I thought I could successfully run away from her, she comes chasing after me.

"Oh. Hey," I gripe. I absolutely do not want to talk to her. I already know why she's here.

"Hey," she replies, puzzled. "What are you doing out here?"

With an irritated sigh, I lean to sit upright, legs crisscrossed. I have to reaffirm my choice, no matter how much it will hurt both of us. "Just thinking about stuff with Tessa."

Marie nods lips in a tight line. "Right. Tessa. Always about Tessa."

"Things are off like I've told you," I begin.

"Yes, you have," Marie fails to hide her irritation in her tone.

"We mainly email because she never has time for video chatting," I continue, ignoring her attitude. "She hasn't ended her emails with 'I love you' since she moved, and I'm afraid I'm losing her. She says she's happy and –"

"Oh my god, give it up!" Marie suddenly yells at me, flapping her arms in an exasperated manner. I flinch in surprise. Marie never shows frustration or anger this way, and it throws me off.

"W-what?" I stutter.

She leans forward on her knees, shoving her hands through her hair. Then she springs to her feet. "Have you thought that maybe she, I don't know, doesn't feel the same way about you anymore, and she's scared to say it? I mean, she very well could have met someone else by now. Have you thought about that? Why haven't you guys just broken up? Your feelings have clearly changed! You *kissed* me, for god's sake! I thought you made your choice to be with me when you stole my first kiss, yet you still can't let her go!"

I was her first kiss. That means her ex never kissed her. I stole that milestone from her. I was too selfish to stand my ground, and I wasted her first kiss.

I have to let her go. I can't ruin her more than I already have.

"First off, Tessa wouldn't do that," I argue through my teeth. "Secondly, I told you that shouldn't have happened. You know I love Tessa; you know she's my girlfriend, so I don't understand why you're not getting that through your head."

"It's not good enough because it doesn't make any sense!" she yells even louder now. "You're so delusional, and you have no idea what you're doing!"

"I know what I'm doing," I stand my ground. "I'm being a loyal boyfriend."

Marie stays rooted in place, staring daggers at me. Wordlessly, she slowly shakes her head, tears begging to stream down her cheeks. Angry, she grabs her backpack off the ground and stomps away.

I don't chase after her. I don't call out to her. I do nothing. Like the coward I am.

"What's gotten into you?" Mason investigates when he comes over to my house later that afternoon. "Didn't see you all day today."

"Just trying to keep my distance," I say with remorse.

"Let me guess. From Marie. Again." I can hear the eye roll in his voice.

I don't answer. Instead, I stare at the microwave as it heats up pizza rolls; every part of my body tensed up.

"You need to let Tessa go," he advises me.

"No," I say brusquely. I can't believe he had the nerve to suggest that.

"You know," I hear the kitchen chair scrape across the floor as Mason stands up. "You're really pissing me off."

I whip my head in his direction. "*You're* pissed off? Are *you* the one trying to do what's right? Are *you* the one trying to figure out how or what to feel?"

"The answer is right in front of you, bro!" he roars at me, infuriated. It's very rare for Mason to yell unless he's excited, so his yelling at me in anger is even more unsettling. "It's right in front of you, yet you're so blind to it that you choose to ignore it, and it's causing problems that could have been avoided a long time ago. All because you feel you have to prove something you never needed to prove!"

"You, of all people, should know why this is important to me!" I scream back. I don't typically yell or scream. Now, I've done it with two important people in my life, and it upsets me, but I've had enough.

"But it's hurting the people around you! You've hurt someone who did nothing to deserve this; you're refusing to listen to the people who actually care about you and want to help you, and yet you can't seem to let go of the one person who won't even pay attention to you! It's *exhausting*, man!"

We stare at each other for what seems like minutes, neither one of us backing down. The microwave beeps, signaling our snack is ready.

"You can have them," Mason says, defeated. "I'm done here."

Mason marches across the living room, shaking his head. He doesn't even bother putting his shoes on. He picks them up and leaves without looking back at me.

When you fall in love, you don't just let them go because it's convenient. You don't let them go because you're the only one who feels it's not going to work out in the end. Tessa hasn't let go, so why should I? What will it take for anyone to understand that?

With the plate of pizza rolls, I sit at the table and eat them one by one. Alone.

I find myself alone the next day. Sitting in my writing place at the brick garden, my notebook lies open on my lap. Yet, I can't think of anything new to write about. My mind jumbles with excessive thoughts. So much so that I can't focus on expanding on my forest story. Now that I have to cut Marie off, I won't have her to help me.

"You!" I hear a girl shout in rage.

I look up from my notebook and find Marie charging at me with the fury of a bull, to the point that it produces fear in me. She violently drops her backpack to the ground with a loud thud on the brick.

"I'm done crying over you!" she shouts while her fist flies at my face. My head whips back from her mighty fist. I know my nose is bleeding from the warmth trickling down my lip. I tumble down to the ground, arms and legs searching for something to hold onto to ease the fall, but I fall flat.

"What the –" I hear Mason shout. Eventually, a large group of students forms, with Mason, Harmony, and Carrie getting front-row seats for the entire scene. Both glower at me, arms folded, doing absolutely nothing to help me out of this situation.

I stay on the ground and hold my hands up. "Marie, what's —"

"SHUT UP!" she screams at me at the top of her lungs. "Just stop talking and shut up for once!"

Her screaming has me stunned and extremely worried. Tears fall down her face in full force. All I can do is let her talk because my mouth can't form any words. I have never seen Marie unleash like this, and my heart breaks seeing her in such agony.

"I thought I could handle being your friend," she seethes through her cries. "I have listened to you, repeatedly, talk about how you love someone else, knowing how I feel about you. And, because I'm stupid, I let you because the thought of losing you was excruciating. Turns out, it's even worse hearing how you'd rather be with someone else when it's not me."

Marie picks up her backpack that she threw on the ground and slings it over her shoulder. Students start to murmur in the background, watching everything unfold before them. Being the guy who got beat up by a girl, this should be hugely embarrassing, but I'm too stunned to feel anything.

"You've done nothing but make me feel like an idiot," she spits at me. "I tried so hard to get you to see that I was someone who wanted to be with you. Someone who was standing right here, giving you my heart, who wanted to be yours and only yours." She shakes her head, a sob blubbering out of her. "This whole time, I thought I actually meant something to you. Instead, I ended up falling in love with you, and you kicked me to the curb. Thanks for nothing."

Marie marches into the school, Carrie at her heels. Being the protective best friend she is, Carrie doesn't fail to give me one more death glare before she's out of sight. I barely notice it, though, because I'm still in shock from the entire scene. Marie not only admitted the heartache I've caused her, but she also confessed her deepest secret.

She's in love with me. Because I've caused her so much pain, she's done with me.

Mason takes a few steps in my direction, arms folded, staring me down. The silence that sits between us is as unsettling as Marie's screaming. To my own surprise, he bends down to help me to my feet.

"Thank you," I mutter.

"Whatever, Seth," he says in a clipped tone, pointing to the direction of the entrance. "You need to make this right with Marie."

I shake my head. "Not now. She's pretty mad at me."

"Can you blame her? Talking about Tessa with her, knowing how she feels about you. That's cold, man." He shakes his head.

"She wanted to stay friends, so I talked to a friend about Tessa! So sue me!"

"I don't know what happened to your common sense, but you don't go talking about how you feel about someone else to the one who has feelings for you. Even I know that's low." Mason moves to walk away, but not before he turns back to say one last thing. "You're on your own with this one. I'm out."

I grind my molars and glare at him, thinking of something to say in return, only to come up with nothing. Instead, I watch my best friend as he grabs Harmony's hand, and go into the school together. Everyone I've cared about has walked away from me, and I have never felt more alone.

"I'm worried about you, Seth," Mr. Nichol says as he stares out the window at the impeccable view of the bay. Brows knitted in worry, he turns and takes a seat across from me at the round table in his office.

It's not the first time I've heard that.

Since everything blew up with Marie a couple of months ago, everything in life has lost meaning. Marie refuses to talk to me. My well of writing ideas has dried up. Conversations with Tessa are without substance. Mason doesn't fail to scowl at me and turn the other direction. My dad has run out of patience to lecture me yet again, so he just scoffs and walks away. I've let down the people I care about most, and I carry that burden with me every day. Marie most of all.

I hurt her deeply. I made the choice to stick to Tessa, and it cost me our whole friendship. No more sitting together. No more card games before school. No more writing notes to each other. No more terrible accents. No more listening to music together.

How did I end up here?

"I know," I grunt out, focusing on the carpet.

Mr. Nichol leans forward, hands clasped in front of him. "Listen, Seth. I've tried being patient with you, and giving you options, but you've chosen to ignore them, so I'm going to have to give it to you straight. Either you catch up on all the work you didn't do this semester – assignments, projects, and finals, all of it. Or you accept the fact that you're not graduating this year, and you're going to have to repeat your senior year after the summer break."

As if it couldn't get worse than this, everyone has given up on me. Even the freaking counselor.

"I really urge you to make the right choice, Seth," he continues. "Is this who you imagined you wanted to be when you grew up?"

I didn't have a good response to that question, so I nodded at him. "Okay. Thank you," I mumbled, then grabbed my backpack and left his office.

Once I get home, the first thing I do is call Tessa. Tessa is all I have left. Even though she's slipping away from me, I would hate myself if I didn't give it my all and try my best to hang on. I need to hang on to *something*. Everything that means the most to me has slipped through my fingers, and it feels beyond my control. I hate myself for it.

"Hello?" Tessa's dad answers the landline in his deep, soft-spoken Morgan Freeman voice. I don't bother calling her cell phone anymore. She hardly ever calls me back anyway.

"Hi, Mister Copeland. Is Tessa there?" I pace my bedroom with my flip phone to my ear.

He sighs, not even shielding his annoyance. "No, she just left. Can I take a message?"

"Just tell her to call me, please. Thank you," I breathe out in a panic.

"Will do, Seth."

I hang up and pace my room even faster. Tessa has officially forgotten she has a boyfriend. Where is she? What's going on? Why is she leaving me hanging like this?

My breathing turns erratic and angry. In the corner of my eye lies my notebook and some other papers. My writing well has turned up dry since I lost Marie. Another reason I hate myself. I can't write. I have no inspiration. I have no one to blame but myself for it.

In one swift movement, I grab the notebook and papers and throw them against the nearest wall with all the strength I have in me. Papers fall everywhere on the floor, mixing with the mess that is in my bedroom. Breathing deeply, I stare at the result of my anger, thinking about the misery that my life has become –

Until a blue folder catches my eye. Where did I get that folder?

Marie's story.

I never read it.

I kneel to the ground, move my paper scraps to the side, and pick up her story. She gave this to me months ago, even though I practically begged her to give it to me. Yet I procrastinated and set it aside. I never gave it a chance.

This is a telltale sign that I'm an awful friend and an awful person.

Is this who you imagined you wanted to be when you grew up?

Mr. Nichol's question rings in my mind.

No. The answer is no. Growing up, I had hopes and dreams like every other kid. I wanted to be a writer. Maybe even teach writing courses. I wanted to publish a story or a book. I wanted to go to college. I wanted to live in a dorm with Mason and be each other's awkward wingman. I wanted to graduate, get married, and maybe have a couple of kids.

Think about what you want your end goal to be.

Marie told me that when we went to Tully's for the first time together.

I run my fingers over the folder, a sad smile creeping on my lips. Memories of Marie flood my brain, and the agony I've become so familiar with comes right with it. Everything I miss about her flashes before me. Her smile. Her laugh. Her love of Snickers. Her hard work ethic. Her kindness. Her green eyes that pierce into my soul.

Now, I know what I want my end goal to be.

Everything I wanted growing up never changed. I want to be a writer. I want to publish a story or a book. I want to go to college and graduate. More than that, I want my dad to be proud of me. I want a close group of friends that all have each other's back.

I want to *live*. For the last year, I haven't been living. I've been surviving.

Marie talked about how it felt to do your best. To feel accomplished. Unfortunately, my mother emphasized something similar until she left, and her life advice dropped dead. Therefore, I used that as an excuse to do nothing. Marie's advice rings in my mind.

Just because your mom left doesn't mean her words have no value.

I turn my head to my backpack that lays on my messy bed. It calls to me to take action. Waiting for me to get my life back together.

With renewed determination, I march over to my backpack on my bed, dig out my textbooks, and slam them on my desk. I have a whole school year of catching up to do.

Once everything is done, I'm giving Marie's story the attention it deserved a long time ago.

"Why don't you take a minute to, I don't know, breathe?" my dad suggests when I grab a fourth cup of coffee on Sunday evening. "Maybe blink a few times?"

During the next few days and over the weekend, I sent a lot of emails to my teachers, asking them to give me every single assignment from the semester that I never turned in. I pulled some all-nighters until my eyes felt like they would turn to raisins, but I kept going. Before school, during lunch, and into the evening. I worked harder than I ever had in my life.

I've been so desperate to finish my homework that I decided to drink some of my dad's coffee to stay awake. If you've learned anything about me, I don't drink coffee. It's disgusting. Nevertheless, desperate times call for desperate measures. Now I'm paying for it with jitters and bloodshot eyes.

"Can't. I need to finish this stuff so I can turn it in tomorrow," I reply with a mug in my hand, the jitters making my entire body shake.

"You have some time before graduation, man," Dad notes. "You can take a break and sleep."

"I'll sleep when I'm done," I grumble as I make my way back up the stairs, coffee in hand.

I sit back down at my desk and look at my History assignment. I'm drained, I'm jittery from all the caffeine, and my eyes want to shut and get some sleep. My body can't decide if it wants to sleep or to stay awake.

Nope. I'm staying awake. I have to do this.

I have to.

Mrs. Buhler freezes when I hand her a stack of paper, eyes bugged out. She remains speechless when she sees the atom bomb of assignments I hand to her.

"You did all of this in a week?" she gasps out.

"Yes," I say apologetically. "Miss Buhler, I'm sorry it took so long to get it to you. And I'm sorry you have to go through each one and grade it. But I want to graduate, and I hope this will get me there."

I watch Mrs. Buhler fumble with the papers and flip through each one. My handwriting is on every single line, on every single piece. Once she's satisfied with what she sees, she peers up at me with a proud smile. "All that matters is you made the effort. Good job, Seth."

Tamping down the smile that begs to show, I turn and step back to my desk. Mrs. Buhler's reaction was totally worth it. Instead of disdain, she had the expression of pride and joy. I can only hope that my other teachers will react the same way.

I lift my gaze to Marie, who quickly turns her head away from my direction and pays close attention to her desk. She still notices me. She's the one who cut me off, but somewhere in there, I can only hope she still cares about me. She does the same thing in my other classes as well, but she seems more captivated by the sudden change in my attitude. She doesn't bother to ask me about it, though—a telltale sign of where our friendship is.

With Mr. Niendorf, I just emailed him everything I hadn't done the whole semester. The only words I put in the body of the email were "I'm sorry." The two words I've been saying to all of my teachers. At least the response I've gotten is a smile or a wink of appreciation.

Marie was completely right. The sense of accomplishment is refreshing. I can, at last, be proud of myself. Little does she know that she's a big reason why I'm trying to be better at all.

This is just one improvement I've knocked out. I know I have more work to do.

"You sure you're ready for this, son?" Dad asks me, very uncertain about what I'm about to do.

We sit in my car, parked in front of a small office building, staring at the front doors. Particularly the front doors to a therapist's office.

For many months, I rejected the idea that I needed help not just with my relationship with my mom but also with my attitude in life. I thought I was content surviving and going through the motions. I've lived in denial for too long.

Marie told me that going to therapy was not a sign of weakness and that it was a sign that a person wants to get better. After losing her and Mason and knowing

I wasn't going to graduate, something had to give. I've been ignoring everything everyone has been trying to tell me.

I need to get better.

"Yes," I answer with finality. "I should've done this a long time ago."

"And I'm proud of you," he reassures me, shaking my shoulder. "She may tell you things you don't want to hear, but she will help you. I promise." He unbuckles his seatbelt. "Now, let's pay this woman to solve our problems."

With a chuckle, we get out of the car and walk towards the double doors, ready to knock out the next step in getting my life in order.

For an hour, Dr. Thurman reaffirmed everything people have been telling me, not just about my mom, but also how I've handled my relationship with Tessa. She had little to offer when it came to what was possibly going through Tessa's mind, but she did advise that I take some time to evaluate and be brutally honest with myself on what I really wanted out of this relationship and accept it. Also, I have to think hard about what Marie means to me and be brutally honest with myself about that as well. In the end, she told me relationships can't be forced to work out. Sometimes, one relationship can teach us valuable lessons that we can take to the next relationship, and I have to understand that that's okay.

When it came to my mom, she told me that I couldn't live in resentment forever if I wanted to have any sort of relationship with her later in life. She advised that the next time she messages me, I offer to meet up with her, hear her out, and go from there.

Mom gave me that open door when she messaged me later that evening.

Debra: I just wanted to say once again that I miss you. In fact, each time I don't hear from you, I cry myself to sleep. We used to be so close, Seth. I miss talking the way we used to.

I repeat in my mind what the therapist said. *Hear her out, and go from there.*

Seth: Hey mom. I'm sorry for how I've treated you. Let's meet for coffee soon. In my case, hot chocolate ☺

It turns out that the result of my letting go was a positive one. Now, I look forward to seeing how coffee will go.

"All right, everyone, finals are here!" Mrs. Buhler claps much too happily as she rounds the room back to her desk. "Just one more step till you can escape."

Students cheer and high-five each other. I would join in the cheer, but I'm crawling with nerves. I hate presenting. We're days away from graduating now, and I still have yet to talk to Marie. It kills me that we may go through graduation and never see each other again.

I don't want that. I *can't* have that.

"Who wants to go first?" Mrs. Buhler's eyes scan the room. "Remember, the sooner you go, the sooner you can get it out of the way."

Nobody says anything for what feels like hours. I want to get this over with as much as the next guy, but I'm waiting to see if anyone will offer first. I go to raise my hand, then –

"I'll go," Marie beats me to it. She looks exhausted with the dark circles under her eyes.

"Okay, go ahead." Mrs. Buhler gestures to the whiteboard.

Eyes glued to the ground, Marie grabs her project and goes to the front of the room. She faces the class with a deep, anxious breath.

"I picked Romeo and Juliet," she begins quietly. "Seems so obvious what the theme of this is, right? Love."

My stomach sinks. I have a feeling I'm going to feel like utter garbage at the end of this presentation.

Keeping her focus on Mrs. Buhler sitting among the students, Marie keeps speaking with more gusto. "I'm going to go out on a limb here and guess that all of you know what happens in this play. Tragic, really. Boy meets girl; they fall in love and get married. In the end, they both die. It's a crappy ending if you ask me. But I've learned something from it."

She starts to choke up but swallows it down. I focus on her entirely, my heart breaking as she keeps herself from breaking down in tears. "Love can be the most euphoric, beautiful thing ever. But, sometimes, it's painful. That pain can crash down on you unexpectedly. I mean, Romeo killed himself because he thought the love of his life was dead. This alone shows how much pain he was in at the idea of losing her. She clearly felt the same way because she killed herself, too. Waking up to find him gone forever was too much to handle."

It's clear as day now. She's directing this final to me. She's sending subliminal messages through this presentation.

I shift in my seat uncomfortably, feeling myself getting emotional with her. I can relate to her. As much as I have focused on my own self-improvement, it's been awful knowing she's not in my life anymore. Just like Juliet, it's almost been too much to handle.

Sniffling, she keeps going, "But when you lose someone you love, whether you were together or not, it feels like it would feel better to be dead. Not to be morbid, but that's the truth of it. And really, there's nothing that hurts more than that."

Marie chokes back a sob. "So" – she quickly wipes the tears from her eyes – "How does this apply to us today? Well, I can say from experience that love is an amazing feeling. Beautiful. Essential for existence. Who would any of us be without it? Sometimes, showing love to each other brings out the best in us. The parts of us that were hidden. And when you find someone who does that for you" – she bravely looks me dead in the eye – "don't let it go."

The class remains silent, their faces in awe of her speech. She still loves me, but she's still hurting from all this. Hurt that I caused her. Hurt that is evident in the exhaustion of her eyes. I want to hold her and make it better. The ache in my chest turns into a stabbing pain, enveloped in gloom.

"Thank you, Marie," Mrs. Buhler says. "Do you need a minute?"

Pursing her lips, she nods vigorously and closes her presentation. Without another word, she keeps her head down and heads straight out to the hallway. She ends up staying out there for the rest of the class. I do my presentation, but it doesn't feel right when I do it when she's not there to see it.

The bell rings, and I pack my stuff. I wait for everyone else to leave the classroom, hoping I can give Marie space and time to get her stuff and leave.

That is until she bumps right into me, trying to get in the classroom. My heart skips a beat, and I'm reminded of the first day we met. My body refuses to step aside as everything that reminds me of her comes back to me in a swift rush.

Her skater shoes.

Her hair in that mid-ponytail.

Her twinkling green eyes.

Her heart-stopping smile.

Her scent that is so flawlessly Marie.

God, I missed her so much. I still do. It kills me that she's so broken because of my thoughtless actions. She's not the same bright personality I grew to love, and it's my fault.

"Are you okay?" I ask in a stupid attempt to show that I still care about her.

Marie freezes, surprised that I have spoken to her for the first time in months. She frantically combs her hair behind her ear, avoiding my gaze. "I'm fine," she replies quietly. Her sweet voice makes my heart skip a beat again. I forgot how much I loved listening to it.

I stand there for a moment, then heave a frustrated sigh. I'm tired of all this – the tension, the silent treatment, this Mexican standoff, the waiting game of who will decide to make the first move. I'm done with it all.

Not saying anything more, I step around her and make my way down the hallway. The hallway we used to walk down together, where we shared laughs and story ideas. Where she dropped her stuff, and I helped make her day a little better.

Missing Marie and our memories causes me to pick up her story and read it after school. At last, I have no drama or mental interruptions, so I'm able to give it my undivided attention.

Princess Heidi's face expresses a look of determination as she watches Daniel suit up for battle. She wants to fight, too, even if it's against her father's orders. Normally, a princess does not fight. This one does, and she absolutely will.

After everyone emptied out of the castle area, Heidi sneaks into the weapons chamber and grabs a bow and some arrows. She makes haste for the stable, where she finds her bright white noble steed, the look of royalty itself. Her horse's eyes are quizzical as Heidi marches up to her with a saddle, flapping it over the horse's back.

Heidi's mouth curved faintly into a grin. She strokes the horse's snout and whispers, "if they want to fight, then let's fight."

After mounting her horse, Heidi wastes no time in galloping at full speed out of the stable, across the castle town, and through the castle gates. Out in the open field, she sees the knights in a battle with the neighboring land that has been hell-bent on conquering their land. Her land.

She finds Daniel about to be knocked off his horse. Even more determined to fight this battle, Heidi raises her bow, aims an arrow at the enemy attacking him, and shoots him straight in the chest. Daniel follows the direction the arrow came from, gratefulness in his eyes.

He watches her pull out another arrow in a swift move and continues shooting.

Her story is amazing. With the evident love triangle and action scenes it captivated me. Marie has a gift.

I hope one day that I can tell her that.

"I can say with complete certainty that you will walk that platform," Mr. Nichol twists in his chair from his computer, completely enthusiastic. "Your GPA shot from 1.0 to a 3.9. Congratulations, you're graduating with your class!"

I remain in a dreamlike state. This entire school year, all these months, I accepted the fact that my graduation was not going to happen. I accepted that my future had nothing to it. All I focused on was surviving and maintaining what little connection I had left with Tessa. Now, I put in a few weeks of hard work to get caught up, and now things are looking brighter.

"Thank you, Mister Nichol." I stand up with my backpack and extend my hand. "For everything."

Out of all the people in my life, he never gave up on me, and I lacked appreciation for that all this time. This is my lame way of saying "Thank you" and "I'm sorry." Two words that I have said a lot lately.

With a slight smile, Mr. Nichol gives my hand a firm shake. "Take care, Seth. Best wishes."

Relief courses through me. All the hard work I put into getting school situated has paid off. I get to graduate with my class. I get to walk that platform and grab that diploma, defeating all odds. I can say I will make my dad proud when he hears this. It's time to pull out my cap and gown.

Wanting to make this moment of relief last, I walk out of the school, across the courtyard, and stand at the S in the middle. I lift my head to the sky, let the sun beat down on my face, and take a couple of deep breaths. I'm relieved, but I still feel a level of loneliness and yearning. The two people I want to share this with the most aren't on speaking terms with me. That sad revelation is interrupted when my phone vibrates in my pocket.

"Hello?" I answer without looking at the caller ID.

"Seth? It's Tessa."

I'm stuck in place. My girlfriend, the one I've been waiting to hear from for months now, has finally, *finally* called me back.

"Tessa?" I gasp. "How are you –?"

"I'm in town with my parents till tomorrow," she cuts in with a tremor. "I was hoping we could meet up at Starbucks. We have to talk, and it's not a conversation I want to have over the phone."

A part of me feels scared, but whatever this conversation leads to, it's been a long time coming. "How soon?"

"I can be there in half an hour."

The moment she says that I'm sprinting across the courtyard.

CHAPTER 13

I make it to Starbucks in Federal Way and hurry inside. I don't even know if I locked my car, nor do I care. I haven't seen my girlfriend in six months; my car is the least of my worries.

I scan the seating area, trying to find a girl who wears all-black clothes, a beanie, and thick-rimmed glasses. I'm unable to find anyone that resembles that appearance. That is until my eyes land on someone who looks very similar to Tessa but is vastly different.

There, at the window where we sat on our first date, is a girl I don't recognize anymore. Glasses are missing from her face as the sun beats down on her. Her hands are clasped around a paper coffee cup, and her nails are covered in blue nail polish instead of black. Instead of a black beanie, her sleek brunette hair is down in waves just past her shoulders, and long bangs lay softly over one side of her face. A light blue tank top, white Toms shoes, and white cut-off shorts replace the black clothing that was commonly present in her outfit choices.

Appalled, I gape at the girl I call my girlfriend. She went through a massive makeover that made her even more beautiful, but a huge contrast to the Tessa I met last year. I approach her at a steady pace, taking her in. She must hear me because she turns to me with a bright, happy smile. The kind of smile I didn't see much of when I met her. Words stick to my throat. It's hard to believe this is the same Tessa I fell for.

"Hey, Seth," she says solemnly and stands up from her seat. Her outfit gives me a view of her body that I never got to see in our relationship. Slender, tan legs, flat stomach, skinny build, and very little makeup that makes her chocolate brown eyes pristine.

"Hey, Tessa," I whisper in astonishment. My arms wrap around her waist as she gets on her tiptoes and hugs my neck. She smells like strawberries and vanilla, something she never had when we were together. She always had a scent that was specifically Tessa, and I loved it.

She lets me go and sits down. No make-out session, not even a peck on the cheek. I would think couples who haven't seen each other in months would be desperate for each other. This is similar to friends meeting up to settle a disagreement.

Something is wrong.

"You look good," she breathes out nervously. "Tired, but good."

I chuckle softly. "I'm very tired. You look good, though. Happy."

"I am. Which is why I called you." She lays her hands out on the table and takes another nervous breath. "There's no easy way to say this, so I'm just going to come out and say it."

Something bad is coming. Her uneasy demeanor, the way she's going into this, there's nothing exciting about any of it.

"I've been seeing someone else," she says quickly.

Time stops. My heart drops, and forgets how to work. I forget how to breathe. The noise in the coffee shop turns into a dull silence. I'm full of questions that all want to pour out at the same time.

She's been seeing someone else? How long has this been going on? Is this why she's been so distant? Why didn't she tell me?

"I didn't mean for it to happen." Tessa blinks back, the tears forming in her eyes. "I missed you so much. I was lonely. I was at rock bottom, and I just lived in my bedroom. I figured this was what my life was supposed to be. Then, I met some girls in my Art class, and they just immediately took me in. They were there for me, encouraged me, didn't give up on me. I felt like I was finally seeing light at the end of the tunnel. Then I met Patrick, and he brought me out of rock bottom."

I stare at her in disbelief. Here is a girl I thought would never even think of letting someone into her protective heart, someone who was always afraid I would leave her, yet that's what has been happening for a few months. I was so determined to believe she would never do this to me, but she proved me wrong.

Marie was right all along.

"Tessa." I start with a scoff. "I was there for you. Even with the distance, I tried. I was loyal to you. I lost sleep over you. I lost friends over you. I fought to the death for you." My voice increases to anger. "Yet you couldn't pick up the phone and tell me you didn't want to be a part of this anymore." I scoff again and rake my hands through my hair. "Why didn't you tell me?"

"I was scared and ashamed," Tessa divulges through tears, avoiding eye contact with me. "You were trying so hard to be loyal to me, and I knew I wasn't doing my part in that. I didn't know how to tell you. And I thought if I just slowly slipped away, maybe got you to move on to someone else, I wouldn't feel so bad for what I was doing."

My head whips up. All of it makes sense now – her indifferent emails, avoiding my phone calls, not telling me she loves me. The puzzle pieces click in place.

"That's why you were trying to get me to date Marie."

Keeping her gaze on her hands, she nods. In her hunched posture, lack of eye contact, and tears, there's a lot of remorse there. How she carried that burden around for months and said nothing, I have no idea.

That leaves only one question.

"Are you in love with him?"

Tessa purses her lips and wrings her hands in front of her chest, studying the table. "Very much so."

I blow out a harsh breath and turn my gaze to the window. All of this is so overwhelming. My girlfriend has fallen in love with someone else. Her entire physical appearance has changed, even the way she smells. Her smile is sincere and cheerful.

She's happy. Not because of me. It all happened right under my nose, and I refused to see it.

"He's helped me a lot," she adds. "He's been helping me with school. I was able to graduate high school last month, and he helped me figure out where I wanted to go to college. He's treated me so well."

"And I didn't?" I'm beyond offended at this comparison game.

"That's not what I'm saying at all," Tessa reassures me when she takes my hand in hers. "You treated me very well. But Seth," she pauses and prepares to say the next stinging statement. "We weren't good for each other."

"How's that?" I sneer.

Tessa sighs. "Once I met Patrick, I realized I needed someone who would motivate me to be a better version of myself. To do better. To be a better person." She gives my hand a consoling squeeze. "Seth, we didn't do that for each other. If anything, we just encouraged each other's behavior. The foundation of our relationship was surface-level and based on crappy attitudes about the world around us. I needed something...more."

Looking back, Tessa is right. We had little in common other than resentment and having creative minds. Our relationship was always surface-level, and I made myself be okay with it because I had something to prove to myself, and I was going to prove it as long as I could.

Patrick motivated her to be a better person. He changed her into the person she is now. She found someone that was better for her.

That sounds familiar, as if that's what has been happening to me.

When I found Marie's story in my bedroom, I remembered how much she cared about doing well in school and how she was trying to get me to see things from a different perspective. Now, I'm graduating high school, talking to my mom again, and going to therapy.

She's the one that changed me for the better.

"Are you okay?" Tessa asks in a comforting tone.

I ponder that question. There was a point in time when I didn't think I could live without her. I loved her so much that I needed her more than my next breath. Right now, however, I feel nothing. I'm numb. Not the kind of numbness that will eventually rear its ugly head in the form of deep grief, but the kind of numbness where I'm not heartbroken. I'm angry with myself for being such a fool and so blind to what was going on behind the scenes, but I'm not hurt.

Which means my heart and focus has been on something else.

Someone else.

"Yeah." I nod slowly. "Yeah. I am."

With a smirk, Tessa leaned back in her chair and crossed her arms and legs to challenge me. "So, what's really going on with you and Marie?"

The subject of Marie causes a strong throb in my chest. I miss her more and more every day. "She's not talking to me right now."

"Why?"

God, I wish I didn't have to repeat this story. I study the table, not wanting to see her facial expression when I tell her. "Long story short, she told me she liked me. I told her I wanted to stay friends, and that went okay until I kept talking to her about you. Then I kissed her."

Tessa's eyes widen in surprise. "You kissed her."

"I know," I groan. I plant my face in my hands in misery of the memory.

"Well, I don't feel quite as bad now," she laughs at herself.

"Even so, I told her I chose you." My cheeks heat in shame. "She punched me, told me she was in love with me, and that she couldn't handle being my friend and listening to me talk about you. We haven't talked since."

"Oh god," Tessa groans out, cringing on my behalf. "Have you tried talking to her?"

I pick at my fingers. "Not really."

Tessa rests her chin on her hand and studies me with a knowing face. "You miss her, though, don't you?"

It feels weird to be talking about missing another girl with someone I once claimed to love more than anything and anyone. We've moved from being a romantic couple to being friends in a matter of minutes. Talking about missing someone to my girlfriend is a weird concept.

Tessa already knows the answer to her own question. Lying to her is useless.

"Yeah," I whisper longingly. "I really do."

"So why don't you try talking to her?" Tessa asks, annoyed.

"I thought she wanted to keep things this way." I shrug. "I figured maybe she was better off without me. That she would be in less pain without me in her life."

Tessa knits her brows, skeptical. "Really? You didn't think she'd want you to talk to her? That's what every girl wants the guy to do when they screw up."

All the reasons I miss Marie flash before me, and it brings a smile to my face. Before I knew it, I spilled out my heart. "You know, every day since I met her, I've looked forward to seeing her. Swapping story ideas, emailing each other, listening to each other's music, walking out of school together. She has this gorgeous, contagious smile that lights up a room and a beautiful laugh." I go downhearted. "Nothing has felt the same since she walked away from me."

"Hmm." Tessa tries to contain her smile. "And you've felt this way since you stopped being friends with Marie?"

"Yeah," I nod in answer.

"Seth," she states pointedly. "You're in love with her. You've *been* in love with her."

You've been in love with her.

Those six words ring in my ears. Is that what I've been feeling this whole time? Not just missing a friend, but being in love with her?

When I fell in love with Tessa, I knew it was love without a doubt. I missed her constantly. I missed kissing her. I was okay just watching movies and going to Starbucks all the time as long as I could be with her. I loved when she helped me with my story or when I gave her my input on her drawings. When she left, I had a sense of yearning. My heart would want to reach out and find Tessa's, only to grasp at the air. Having that kind of unmet longing is an agony I never expected to feel.

When I was becoming closer to Marie, I started feeling the same things I had felt when I first met Tessa, and I brushed it off. The only difference was the unmet yearning felt much, much more powerful with Marie. My heart not only wanted to find Marie's, but my entire being – my *soul* – wanted to find her, hold on, and never let go.

"I know I have feelings for her," I breathe out. "I was so focused on trying to make this work with you that I never let myself feel what I want to feel. It all feels so wrong, but so right at the same time."

"Well, if it makes you feel any better, you can stop holding back now. It's time to accept how you really feel."

Literally, the same thing Dr. Thurman told me. If I have learned anything, if more than one person has said the same thing, it must be true. I have a lot of thinking to do.

Here is my girlfriend – now ex-girlfriend – giving me permission to accept my feelings for someone else. To stop rejecting my emotions. Whatever Tessa's friends, or Patrick, have done to make her change for the better has made her do a complete one-eighty and shine with confidence.

Tessa clears her throat and throws her purse around her shoulder. I stand up with her. "I should get going," she says awkwardly. "I'm sorry about...everything. I should have told you about this from the beginning."

Inwardly, I agreed with her. Otherwise, it wouldn't have been a waste of time holding onto something that had gone extinct. On the other hand, I never told her about having feelings for Marie or that I gave in and kissed her. We both carried secrets. Secrets serious enough to end our relationship.

"Me too," I reply, shoving my hands in my pockets.

Tessa stands in front of me for a moment and searches me with apologetic eyes and a world of blame. She wraps her arms around my waist, leaning her head against my chest. I'm hit with a whirl of memories of how good it felt when I used to hug Tessa, and I hold her tighter, knowing it's the last time I will ever see or hold her.

It's over. It's bittersweet, in a way. It doesn't hurt, and we both know this is for the best. We helped each other to see where we needed to be. We were not the right people to lead each other in the right direction in life. We were not going to be the right match for each other. We grew into different people, and we each found someone who was a better fit for who we needed to be.

Tessa lets go of me and winks. "Time to get your girl back, Harris."

I nod in agreement and grab her shoulders with sincerity. "Thank you."

"For what?"

My lips pull into a smile. "For getting me here."

Tessa grips my shoulders in return, showing that she's proud of the man standing in front of her. In a way, I'm proud of myself, too. I've gotten back in line, but I still have work to do.

"Best wishes, Seth," Tessa whispers, tears filling her eyes.

With that, I depart, leaving Tessa and Starbucks behind. Once I got to my car, I looked back at the coffee shop one last time. I have no reason to come back here now that Tessa and I are over. Now, I know if I happen to come in this direction again, I'll always remember that this is where I unexpectedly embarked on a new road in life. This is the place where that road ended.

Now, I have a different road to start.

I have to get my girl back.

Once I got home from Starbucks, I trailed up the steps to the door. I shut it behind me, leaning my back against it. There's a lot swimming in my mind; so much so that I don't even remember driving home.

Dad sits at the kitchen table with a soda can and newspaper. He sees me standing at the door, staring aimlessly at nothing. "What's goin' on?"

With a heavy sigh, I sauntered to the kitchen and sat in front of Dad. "Tessa broke up with me. She was seeing someone else after she moved."

My dad puts the newspaper down and leans forward, making an effort to hide his smirk. "Can't say I didn't see that comin'," he remarks. "Are you okay?"

My brows bunch together, surprised with myself. "I am, actually. Better than I thought I would be."

"Which means this was bound to happen." Dad releases a sigh, signaling that he's about to get serious. "Look, I know what you were tryin' to do with Tessa, but there comes a time when a relationship just will not work, no matter how hard you try. That's what happened with your mom and me."

"What do you mean?"

"When your mom told me she was movin' in with a woman she had been seein', I still tried to get her back. I still loved her, you know. Like you, I did everythin' I could to keep it afloat. Sendin' her flowers, love letters, leavin' voicemails tellin' her I've been thinkin' of her, offered to go to marriage counselin'. I even told her I would go with her to that wine and paint class that she loved so much."

I don't respond at first. Just gaze at him in amazement. I had no idea he worked so hard to get her to stay, even when she changed her mind about how she felt about him.

"I remember the last time I tried," he reminisces. "I was on my knees, in tears. You know me, boy, I don't cry, but I was desperate. Anyhow, I was on the front porch of her girlfriend's house, beggin' her to come back home. She told me she would think about it. When I heard a knock on the door the next day, I thought Debra had changed her mind. It wasn't Debra. It was a lawyer with divorce papers. I knew there was nothin' more I could do. I had to let her go. There was no point in tryin' to revive somethin' that was dead."

He turns to me with a world of pain in his eyes. "My point is, I know what you were feelin'. But, even though you were fiercely loyal, if the other person ain't showin' that same commitment, you're wastin' your breath. Give that effort to someone who truly wants and deserves it."

I take in everything he said, still in disbelief. "Why didn't you tell me any of this?" I question.

"I didn't think you'd listen," he answers. "I also hoped that you would figure it out on your own. I knew you needed to prove somethin' to yourself, but I thought somewhere down the line, you would see that your efforts would be in vain. And learn from it."

I nod in understanding. Again, I say the two words that I have been saying often to the person who needs to hear them. "I'm sorry, Dad. For everything I put you through."

"It's okay." He winks, then gets up to go to the counter.

"I didn't realize you were such a romantic," I point out. "How are you still single?"

"Ha!" Dad barks, sifting through the mail on the counter. "After seein' everythin' you've been through, I think I enjoy bein' single. Less drama." He pulls out an envelope and studies it. "Hey, you got somethin' from the University of Puget Sound."

I hurriedly spring up from my chair to stand. I applied for that college once I was getting my grades back up. I wanted to get a head start on applying for colleges, even though my grades hadn't been posted yet. Puget Sound caught my eye because they had creative writing programs I wanted to get into, and it's close to home, just as my dad wanted. Mr. Nichol had to pull a few strings on my behalf for them to give me a chance.

"Oh, man." I take the envelope with shaky hands. "This will tell me if I got in or not."

"Well, open it, for god's sake!" Dad rubs his hands impatiently.

Even more nervous now, I open the envelope, take out the letter, and skim the contents. My face breaks out into a smile. "I got in."

"Oh, thank god!" he shouts and crashes into me in a bear hug. "Best news I've heard all year!"

Dad catches me off guard when he wraps me in a bear hug. He hasn't hugged me in quite some time. I knew that he loved and cared for me, but he was never the affectionate type. Now, he's hugging me. He's proud of me. Truly proud of me.

Chest swelling with pride, I return the hug. Turns out this was just what I needed. Someone to show me they were still there for me. Victor Harris never failed to do just that, even when he was mad at me. I will always admire him for it.

Dad lets go and claps my shoulder. "Heck, if I knew that all it would take was a girl to get you here, I would've signed you up for eHarmony a long time ago."

I chuckle and shake my head. "No. No more meeting people on the Internet."

Dad laughs for a bit, then turns away from me, sniffling and wiping his eyes.

"You crying?" I ask with a grin.

"No," he says emotionally. "Just tryin' not to sneeze."

He's not a very good liar. My dad never cries. I suppose something has to be important to him for him to cry about it. He might come across as a gruff, tough man, but deep inside the shell of toughness, he's just a teddy bear. I can take pride in knowing that I made him shed happy tears.

"Okay," I say, accepting his answer. "I'm going to tell Mason the good news."

I rush upstairs and open up Instant Messenger. He's avoided me a lot lately, but I know he will be relieved with this news.

Seth: *Dude, you're not going to believe this, but I got into the University of Puget Sound!*

I sent Mason the IM. With everything that's happened lately, I thought I should catch him up. He will no doubt be proud of me.

Mason: *…You did?*

Seth: *I did. My GPA is 3.9 now, I turned everything in from the entire year in all my classes, I've been going to therapy, and I had coffee with my mom the other day, which turned into a two-hour conversation. And Tessa and I broke up.*

Mason:*…*

Mason: *OK…that's a lot to take in. I need a minute.*

Seth:*…*

About five minutes later...

Mason: I took it all in. I have one thing to say. THANK FREAKING GOD! FINALLY, YOU GOT IT TOGETHER!

I can't help it. I throw my head back and laugh. I'm laughing not only because of Mason's reaction but also because I finally feel free.

Seth: Say hello to the new and improved Seth Harris.

Mason: Congrats, man! Class of 2007, here we come!

Mason: So, now the question is, are you gonna talk to Marie?

Seth: Soon. She deserves a grand gesture of some sort. I think I have an idea.

Mason: Let me know if you need help. In the meantime, I've been ignoring Harmony for this conversation. Boyfriend duty calls.

Seth: Understood. Have fun.

Mason: Seriously, I'm glad you got your crap together. Ttyl.

Mason exits the conversation. My laughter takes over again, and I feel so liberated. I broke myself out of the burden of negative feelings and unrealistic expectations. I'm free from it all.

I turn to Marie's story and flip over to where I left off. I want to finish this before we graduate so I can give it back to her.

Daniel lays on the ground, thoroughly exhausted from the fight. James is a talented fighter and warrior, skilled with a number of weapons. Daniel was a newly appointed knight; surely, there was no way he had a chance to win this battle. He was skilled himself, but James was his trainer. He had a leg up all along.

The stadium is silent. James stands a few feet away with the devilish of grins, as if he just hunted down a prized animal, practically begging Daniel to get up and keep fighting. That is, until, he grabs a sword and approaches Daniel, about to finish him off once and for all. Daniel still doesn't move. He has no more fight left in him.

"You thought you could steal my bride. You fool," James spits out.

I love you, Heidi. I'm sorry. Daniel says in his head. He wishes he had it in him to say it aloud, even if she couldn't hear him.

"STOP THIS AT ONCE!" a female voice screams from the side. Everything stops. Everyone's head turns to the source of the screaming.

Daniel manages to turn his head to see Princess Heidi running as fast as her legs will take her across the arena, towards James, hand outstretched and tears running down her face.

"What do you think you're doing?" James snaps at her. "You're interrupting a duel, here!"

"Don't you dare lay another finger on him," Heidi demands. She glowers at him with all the seriousness she has. "I love that man."

"Excuse me?" James bellows. His persona reeks of tyranny at this point.

"I love him, James," she confesses. "Lay down your sword."

"You dare tell me what to do?" James is so angry he nearly foams at the mouth. "You are embarrassing yourself!"

"As Princess of Windsor, I command you to drop your sword, or I shall have you thrown in the town prison." Heidi lifts her head high, showing him who has the real authority. "Even if you won this battle, I refuse to marry the rat of a man that you are, arranged marriage aside. I will tell you once more. Stand. Down."

James shifts his gaze between Daniel and Heidi. Daniel has a radiant smile; proud of the woman he loves standing up for herself. James, on the other hand, hangs his head in defeat. Nothing would humiliate him more than being thrown in prison.

At her command, he drops his sword. The clang echoes in the silent air.

Daniel won. And it's over.

Once I finish Marie's story, I contemplate how long it's been since I've written anything that's had any substance. I miss writing. I've had writer's block since everything went down with her, and I really want to get back into it. I'm desperate to write about something. *Anything*.

I grab my writing notebook, flip it open to the last page I was on, and think. Writers usually advise others to write what they know. I reflect on what I know and what I have experience in. Mysteries, school, friends, divorce, grief, love –

Love. I could write about love. Being in love and losing it.

Newly inspired, I turned back to my notebook, picking up my pen to write, but stopped. It's too quiet in here. I need background noise.

Music.

The playlist on my YouTube account has so much more music compared to what it was at the beginning of the year. It used to be straight-up rock music, now there's eighties music and smooth jazz mixed into the list. The type of music that would make people conclude I'm gay.

There's only one person that has had that much influence on my music.

I click on "Bloom" and let Mindi Abair fill the empty space in my bedroom. I let it play for a few seconds, thinking about whether I want to change it to something else. A memory of Marie flashes in front of me. When she first showed me this song, I got to see firsthand how music affected her. It tugged her heartstrings. It affected her on a much deeper level.

Marie and I had a connection that I never felt with anyone else. We shared the love of the same craft that made us bond from the beginning. We could be our silly selves and have inside jokes that only we understood. She showed me how strong, loving, and hardworking she was. She accepted me for who I was and deeply cared for my well-being.

Tessa may have told me to accept how I feel about her, but I think I've already known for a while.

I love her. I love her with every fiber of my being. I need her, and I'm going to fight for her. It's more intense than the first time I felt it. It's deeper, with a more solid foundation. I became a better, more solid person, telling me this was more real than anything I felt before.

From here, ideas start to flow. I pick up my pen and start writing where I feel most at home.

"What do you want?" Jess snapped at Andy when she opened the door. Andy stood at the doorstep, hands in his pockets. He stared at the ground for a moment before he looked up at her, desperate and heartbroken.

"I love you, Jess," Andy told her, tears collecting in his eyes. He took her hands in his and held them to his chest. "I made some stupid choices, but I don't want to lose you. And if you'll let me, I'll spend every waking moment of my life proving how much you mean to me. Please."

Jess withdrew her hand and choked back a sob. "I don't know," Jess said with a tremor in her voice. "I gave you my heart, and you stomped on it."

Andy sighed and looked away, not able to bear the pain of her words. This may be the last time he'll ever see her, and it's becoming a heartbreaking reality. Death sounds better than the pain in his heart.

"But I love you," she added. "I always have, and I always will."

With a huge sigh of relief, Andy took the woman he loves in his arms and held her, his life depending on her presence. Jess's body shook from her sobs, as she held him just as tightly.

It's the kind of story I don't usually write. There's no father missing his child. There's no suspense. It's about the pain of loss, being in love, and working to make things work with the person you love.

I wrote my own story.

The only difference is I don't know how my story will end. Even worse, I don't know if it will end well.

Give that effort to someone who truly wants and deserves it.

I think about everything Dad just told me. I worked so hard to be loyal to Tessa, who didn't appreciate my loyalty because she found someone else who could physically be near her. Marie, on the other hand, was there the whole time. She gave me her heart, and I handed it back to her like a cold-hearted moron.

Marie deserves that same effort and so much more.

With a sigh, I peer back on her story. If I'm going to fix this, I need to do something big. As someone who has never been through this scenario, I don't think anything I came up with would be good enough.

Now that we're talking again, I know whom I can ask for advice. The other romantic in the family.

Seth: *Hey, Mom, I need your help on something.*

CHAPTER 14

"Line up in pairs, people! Find a partner and line up in pairs!" one of the teachers shouts with a deep, demanding voice. "Memorize the person in front of you so you end up in the right place in line!"

Students scramble to find their positions while I stand off to the side, pondering my next move. The entire senior class had to meet at the Tacoma Dome to rehearse the graduation ceremony. The floor space is bigger than a football field, entirely made of concrete, with the domed ceiling connected and held up with rafters. The makeshift stage is set up on one side of the arena, draped in our school colors, blue and gold. A subtle reminder of how much I look forward to being done with this place.

When I see Marie standing in front of Carrie in line, I realize how much I'm done with this silent game we've been playing for the last few months. With her blue folder and a Snickers bar stuffed inside of it, I hope that game ends now.

Mom told me I should do something sentimental. Something that was special to both of us. Something that only she would understand the meaning behind it. According to Mom, a thoughtful, simple, romantic gesture will probably mean more to Marie than something elaborate.

I wrote her a letter—specifically, a letter on the last page of her story.

It took me most of the night last night to figure out how to write what I wanted to tell her. I wanted her to know everything I was feeling, what I fought to feel, and how she affected my life since I met her. I reviewed it and erased it like crazy, but I did what I could.

I open the folder to the last page, holding the Snickers bar in place, and reread my letter one last time.

```
Dear Marie,
This letter has been a long time coming. Normally,
I would talk to you face to face, but writing each
other notes was kind of our thing, and I want to keep
it that way. I also never paid you back for giving
me your last Snickers bar. Not that it makes up for
anything, but I hope it's a start.
I just want to say I'm so sorry about everything.
I royally screwed up, and I have no one to blame but
myself. I was trying so hard not to give up on Tessa
as my mom did on my dad, but it was all pointless
because she told me a couple of weeks ago that she
was seeing someone else. So, you were right about her.
Either way, I ended up losing the best thing that ever
happened to me: you. However, as excruciating as it's
been not talking to you, I realized I had to get my
life back together, so I took the time to do that.
I've gone to therapy, I'm talking to my mom again,
and now I'm graduating. I've even expanded my writing
to different areas. People on Gaia went nuts over my
last story. You were right about music affecting your
```

writing because that's what I've been doing, and it
helped greatly. Without your wise advice and example
to follow, I probably would have been stuck right
where I was before I met you. You, of all people,
know I was not in a good place. You made me a better
person. Just like your favorite song, I bloomed. It's
all thanks to you.

I've missed you a lot, Katharine Hepburn. And the
idea of walking across that stage, getting that
diploma, and never seeing you again is a sting I don't
want to carry with me through life. I know I hurt you
terribly, and I don't expect you to forgive me right
away, but I hope you can find it in your heart one
day.

I'll wait for you.

Seth, a.k.a Peaches

Satisfied, I close the folder. By the advice of my mom and Carrie, I didn't tell her how I truly felt about her in writing. I want to save that for tomorrow when I talk to her face-to-face about the letter.

I scan the crowd to find Marie. Most of the line has been formed by now. I don't move when I seek out every student in line until I find Carrie, who's giving me a wink. Yes, I reached out to Carrie for help, too. She knows Marie better than anyone. I wanted to do this right. Marie deserves nothing less than that.

Inhaling a sharp breath, I march over to where Marie is standing. She hears me approaching and turns in my direction, but she immediately glares at me and twists her head away from me. She can ignore me all she wants, but I'm not going anywhere.

"Hey Marie," I greet her with a low voice.

"Hey," she replies curtly, pursing her lips and avoiding my eyes.

I hand her the folder with the lump the Snickers bar is creating. "I, uh, just wanted to give you this."

Marie's mouth forms an O as she stares at the folder in disbelief. With a light gasp, she took the folder and opened it to find the candy bar. She fights it, but her mouth turns up on one side. I'm relieved that I got her to smile a little bit. I have a fighting chance here.

"Your story was amazing," I tell her with sadness laced in my tone. If this doesn't work, I may never see her again, and it terrifies me. "I really liked it. You should definitely try to get it published."

Carrie watches Marie with a grin, in a way that tells Marie to take my word for it. "Thank you," Marie says with a quiver.

"I just wanted to give you that," I say awkwardly and take a step back. "And you might want to turn to the last page."

With that, I turn to find my place in line, anxious nerves flowing through me. If nothing changes between us tomorrow, I'll know I'm too late.

That night, as I sat on my bed, staring at the royal blue cap and gown with the gold tassel, all I could think about was the roller coaster this year had been. Crappy grades, falling in love, meeting someone else, trying very hard and failing from falling for someone else, losing both of them, getting my grades up, going to therapy, and improving my relationships all bundled in a ten-month period.

Without all those things happening, I wouldn't be where I am now. I wouldn't see a cap and gown hung up at my door. I would see a blank door with zero opportunities, reliving the same circle I found myself stuck in.

What a pity to think I felt content living that way.

I told Marie I hoped she could forgive me one day, but I sincerely wanted her to do it sooner than later. Now that I have Carrie on my side, she'll vet for me. She told me if this doesn't work, for whatever reason, that I need to keep fighting.

I will fight. Us Harris's fight for what we want.

Suddenly feeling nostalgic, I dig through a pile of developed pictures next to my bed. I pop open the tab on one of the sleeves and take out the pictures. The first picture I see is the self-portrait photo Carrie took of us at the party. Then I flip the one she took when Mason decided he wanted to be a part of the group picture, and I chuckle at the faces he was making that night. After that is a photo of Marie and me, arms wrapped around each other's waists with sincerely happy smiles. It was the most fun I'd ever had, and it was because of her. She was stunning that night. My emotions went into a tailspin, and they never stopped from that moment on.

After a few more pictures that Carrie took of us at the second stage and at the courtyard, I landed on my now favorite picture: Marie and I joyriding in her car. The day she taught me how to drive a stick shift. The day I stopped denying how I really felt about her. The day I kissed her.

I already know I'm not going to sleep well tonight. I'm going to spend most of it wondering how she's going to react to seeing me at graduation now that she knows what I've been going through. At least some of it.

The rest she will no doubt know tomorrow.

"It's goin' to work out, son," Dad claps my shoulder. "It's goin' to be a great day."

Dad and I met up at the front of the Tacoma Dome, where families and students pour into the arena. He wanted to meet up with me to take graduation photos and give me a pep talk before the ceremony, which I'm glad he did because I needed it. In addition, I was meeting up with my mom, and he didn't want to run into her.

"Thanks, Dad," I say as he hugs me once more.

"Now get in there and get your girl back," he waves me off. "Have fun tonight!"

I zip my gown over my black slacks and white dress shirt and make my way into the Tacoma Dome. It's a bright, sunny, and warm day, perfect for what I have potentially planned after this.

I make my way through the sea of my graduating class, hugging each other and laughing. I find Mason waiting for me with the rest of the class.

"Did you find her yet?" Mason inquires.

"No," I answer with desperation, scanning the crowd.

"I think I saw her and Carrie over there," he points to an area behind the stage. "We're lining up pretty soon, so try to be quick."

I go in the general direction of where Mason is pointing, my legs wanting to give out on me.

Marie stands with Carrie and a few other girls, along with Harmony, wearing black heels with her graduation outfit blonde hair highlighted and curled. She's so gorgeous, just standing there. Nothing feels more right than having her by my side, and I'm on my way to fight for that.

"Hey Marie," I greet her. Carrie takes this as her cue, so she motions for the other girls to follow her to hang out somewhere else.

This time, when she looks at me, it's not anger. It's just plain hurt. "Hey," she says softly, lips quivering.

"I take it you read my letter," I shrug and chuckle, keeping the mood light.

"Yeah," she replies, picking at the cap in her hands.

These one-word answers are killing me. "Okay," I drag out. "So, what do you think?"

Marie scoffs and shifts her weight. "I don't know, Seth." She sniffs, keeping the tears at bay.

"Well, then let's talk about it," I beg her, grabbing her elbow. "Please."

She yanks her elbow away from my grasp. "What is there to talk about?"

"Everyone, get into position; we're about to start!" a teacher shouts at the students. "Make sure your tassels are on the right side of your cap!"

I groan in frustration as Marie's eyes gaze at me with pity. Without saying anything else, she puts her cap on her head and walks away, the entire state of our friendship hanging in the air.

Mason appears from behind me. "How did it go?" he asks.

I put my cap on. "She doesn't know."

"Okay, plan B it is," he comments as we get in position in line.

During the ceremony, we walk in pairs to our seats in front of the stage, parents clapping and shouting their support from the stands. I soak it all in, knowing both of my parents are here, cheering me on and showing their pride for their only son.

When the valedictorian gives her speech, I don't even pay attention to what she's saying. I pay attention to Marie's facial expressions, deciphering if she's thinking about me or thinking about anything I've said. She remains stoic in her posture but deep in thought. Impatience is all I'm feeling right now because I'm desperate to finish our conversation.

Two students are at the mike now, performing a song they wrote together. I try blocking out thoughts of Marie and watch the performance, which, quite frankly, is hilarious. I laugh along with the crowd, but I linger in distraction.

Everyone comes to stand, and row-by-row students make their way to the area behind the stage. It's time to receive our diplomas and act out plan B.

"All right, go get her," Mason gives me a high five.

Marie and Carrie stand up ahead, close to the beginning of the line. A staff member has started calling out the students' names, so I need to make this quick before Marie snags her diploma next.

"Hey, Carrie, can I take your place?" I tap her shoulder to ask.

"Of course!" she says in a chipper tone, stepping away from the line. She knew I was going to do this. She and Mason helped me plan this all out.

"No, Carrie!" Marie whisper shouts at her at the same time.

Carrie whispers something in her ear before getting out of line to find Mason. Marie glowers at Carrie's back as she walks away in her stilettos. Now I'm alone with Marie, and I can get this all out in the open.

"So, you didn't answer my question," I begin.

"What question?" Marie seethes. She's so mad her eyes could shoot lasers. "What do you want, Seth?"

"What did you think of my letter?"

"I told you I don't know."

"That's not an answer."

Her tongue rolls over her teeth, and she shoots me a glare. "Well, from the sounds of it, you still just want to be friends, even though things didn't work out with Tessa. I don't know how much clearer you need me to be, but I can't be just friends. So thanks, but no," she spits out at me. She shoves me aside and gets out of line.

"No," I demand, dead serious, grabbing her arm and yanking her back in her place. "We're not done."

"Yeah, I think we are."

Another applause breaks out, and the line moves forward. Marie and I are coming up very soon. I need to get this out quickly.

"No, we're not, Marie. Not even close."

Marie closes her mouth, surprised by the demanding tone of my voice. She stills and waits for me to talk, although impatiently.

"About eight months ago, I met the sweetest, most amazing girl in the hallway outside of English class. And as hard as I tried to deny it, I've been crazy about her ever since."

Marie wonders if what I'm saying is true with the way her brows knit together. I cup her face with my hands, showing her that I'm telling her the whole truth. The line keeps moving forward, the cheers from the crowd becoming the background noise to this moment.

"You were right. I wasn't being realistic. I pushed you away, and I lost everyone that was important to me. Losing you was the worst heartache, and I can't live through that again. I need you by my side, Marie. There's no life without you in it."

Tears fall down her cheeks, lips twisted as she tries to stop herself from crying. I wipe the tears from her eyes with my thumbs, showing her the affection I can give her. The affection she deserves.

"So, what are you saying?" she finally asks mid-cry, wiping under her eyes with her index finger the best she can without ruining her makeup.

I lean my forehead to hers and speak my heart. "I love you, Marie. I've loved you since the moment I saw you in the hallway."

She covers her mouth with her hand and cries. Months and months of emotional turmoil, heartache, and pure joy mix in her subdued sobs, and I continue to lean my forehead on hers. I let her just...feel. Everything we've been through together, good times and bad, stands between us as I wait for her to give her heart another chance. To pick up where we left off. Start a new chapter, with nothing holding me back.

Behind me, Mason and Carrie watch in anticipation, barely containing their smiles. Marie turned in the same direction I was looking, and she started to giggle, figuring out they had a part in making all of this happen.

"Got some outside help, did we?" Marie remarks with a grin.

"Had to do it right."

I didn't notice how much the line had moved until I found myself at the steps leading to the stage. The time has finally come. I worked so hard to get to this point from rock bottom, and now I get to claim my prize. Marie is my next prize, if she'll have me.

I kiss her on the forehead and get up on the steps. "I love you," I whisper to her one more time.

The cheers die down a little bit, and I step all the way onto the stage, completely in the spotlight. I hand the paper with my name on it to the staff member

"Seth Kyle Harris," she enunciates into the microphone.

That announcement is a declaration that I've reached the finish line. The audience erupts in cheers, and I swear I can hear my dad bellowing his deep voice across the entire building. I shake hands with the principal and get my picture taken. Now, I can enjoy the fulfilling sense of accomplishment, just as Marie told me.

"Marie Katharine Burn," the staff member calls out.

As I walked back to the seats, I watched Marie grab her diploma with a tear-stained face. She gapes at it for a moment with a reflective expression. I know that expression. I wore it last night when I examined my cap and gown. She went through so much to get here. She worked her butt off for that diploma, and she finally has it.

I occupy the seat Carrie would have sat in and watch Marie as she turns to the audience and raises the diploma in the air, pumping it like a trophy. The cheers in the audience continue, and it makes me smile until my face hurts, seeing her victorious. She reached the finish line, too.

After she took her photo with the principal, she walked off the stage and sat next to me. I lightly bounce on my feet, apprehensive to know where we stand at this point.

To my surprise, she reaches out and smooths her hand on my cheek, full of bliss, pure affection, and love.

"I love you too, Seth," she tells me, more tears escaping her eyes. "I never stopped."

I bite my lip to contain my own bliss. After all this time, through the bitter anger and hurt, she never stopped loving me. She could have let me go and moved on with her life. But she held on to the hope that we would come back someday. She never let go.

My arms loop around her, and she snuggles into the crook of my arm, my head leaning on hers. For the first time, I'm embracing a woman I truly love. I'm not infatuated with her, or satisfied with the surface-level things. No, this is deep and real. The kind of love that took its time to form into what it is. I take in her smell, the feel of her small frame in my arms. In a silent agreement, we're starting from scratch. In my case, I'm starting over this time with the one I should have been with all along. No regret to follow me everywhere I go. Nothing to hold it against me. Just peace, contentment, and showing love.

As I held my girl, we watched the stage as Carrie's name was announced. She shimmies her boobs and hips before grabbing the diploma. Marie laughs and shakes her head as most of the guys cheer her on louder than everyone else. Carrie has a reputation for being a bit boy-crazy, and clearly, all the guys love it. Then, we watch Mason do a silly dance upon receiving his diploma. Everyone is happy to reach this milestone, and we're all celebrating it together. For me and Marie, we're celebrating the fact that we found our way back.

The principal approaches the podium, telling us it's time to move our tassels over. We all move them from the right to the left, signifying the close of a chapter and opening a new one. I was dreading this moment last night, thinking I would also be closing the chapter on Marie and everything that could have been. We're together for this one, though, and that's even more thrilling.

As if the entire student body had the same idea, we took our caps off our heads and threw them in the air in celebration. As all our caps fly in midair, I take this chance to take Marie in my arms, dip her, and kiss her the way I wanted to kiss her from the beginning: without reserve. She lifts her body closer to me and holds me close as she kisses me back, afraid that something will happen to take this moment away from us.

I'm not going anywhere. I mean it this time.

I bring her back to her feet and kiss her more. I'm finding out very quickly that I'm addicted to her lips. The crowd, including all the students, cheer around us, but we don't hear it. It's just us, finally being together and soaking in the joy.

"Do you have any plans after this?" I ask against her lips.

"Today, no," she answers, arms looped around my neck and holding me close as if I'll somehow vanish from sight.

"Want to go for a drive?" I grin mischievously. "Relive our glory days?"

Her teeth roll over her bottom lip. "You got a sunroof?"

"I do."

"Then let's go."

Marie grabs my hand, and we run toward the exit, being two teens in love. This was exactly what I wanted to happen after graduation, which is why I drove separately. Outside, everyone is taking photos with their family and friends. A woman who looks exactly like Marie waits for us by the street, digital camera in hand.

"My mom will want to take photos," she winces at me. "If I ditch her, she will lose her mind."

My face falls. Crap. That's her mother. I'm already meeting her mother.

"Don't look so excited," she says sarcastically and intertwines her fingers in mine. "Don't worry. This should only take a few minutes."

Suzanne Burn could easily pass as Marie's sister. She has a short stature, blonde hair, and blue eyes, which gives the impression that she's approachable. Marie introduced us, and Suzanne seemed very welcoming but also gave off a protective "mother bear" vibe. Carrie did the same thing when I met her; I'm used to it. There will come a day when I'll let Suzanne know that her daughter means the world to me.

"Marie, be back by nine," Suzanne says to Marie in her motherly tone after we take pictures.

"I know, Mom," Marie replies and gives her a kiss on the cheek. "I love you."

"Love you too, honey," she calls out to us. I found that moment to be endearing, seeing how close she is to Suzanne. It also helps that she seems to approve of me being with her daughter.

Marie takes my hand, and we get to the curb until a girl's voice stops us.

"Wait, Marie!" Carrie shouts for her. She waddles toward us in her heels, straight brunette hair waving with every movement. She grabs Marie's arm and pulls her in for a loving hug. I let them have their moment as they quietly talk to each other. Marie looks at me and combs a strand of hair behind her ear, smiling sweetly before turning back to Carrie.

"You!" Carrie suddenly shouts, finger pointed at me. "If you ever hurt her again, I'll punch you between the eyes and make sure you can't procreate."

I chuckle at her fiery personality, hands in my pockets. "I can assure you that won't happen."

Once Carrie seems to approve, she kisses Marie's cheek. "Make up for lost time. Do everything I would do."

"Obviously," Marie replies with a hint of mischief, and then she takes my hand and crosses the street with me.

We get in my car, acting like little kids with our giggling. Before I put my seatbelt on, I lean over the console and tilt her chin up with my finger, giving her another kiss.

"So where are we going, Peaches?" she says in a sexy, sultry voice.

I rub my nose with hers before kissing her one more time. Those delicious lips are hard to resist. "Don't worry about it."

I start the car, opening all the windows and the sunroof, letting in the sunlight and the light summer breeze of June weather. I make a point to play "Bloom" on the CD player.

"You really do love me!" Marie exclaims, bouncing up and down in her seat.

"I wasn't lying!"

As the sound of Mindi's saxophone fills the space in the car, we leave the parking lot and head over to I-5, where Marie drove us when we rode in her Miata—truly reliving our best memory and holding it close to our hearts.

Once we get on the freeway, Marie takes her seatbelt off, climbs onto the console, and peeks her head out of the sunroof. The summer air blows her hair into a golden river behind her.

"I'm free!" she screams and throws her arms in the air. "I'm free, I'm in love, and I don't care who knows it!"

My laughter carries in the air as we drive toward the horizon. Toward a new beginning. The road to get here was a hard one, but as my father said, one day, I'll look back and be glad I was led in a better direction.

With my girl next to me, ready to take on the road ahead, I don't have to wait years to figure that out. I already know.

Want to listen to the music referenced in this book?

Visit www.sarahblynnewrites.com and find the Spotify playlist curated for

this book in the Shop section!

Follow Sarah on –

Tiktok: @sarahblynne

Instagram: @sarahblynnewrites

Facebook: Sarah Blynne Writes

Feel free to leave a review on Amazon, Goodreads or Barnes & Noble!

ACKNOWLEDGMENTS

Phew! This book has been a long time coming, and it has a special place in my heart, as it's based on real events in my life. After about fifteen years in the making, I'm so grateful I could finally put this out there for the world to read.

First, I would like to thank my parents, Francine and Alex, for one hundred percent having my back with my writing career and giving me advice throughout the process. Mom, you were my rock during my high school years. I would have been lost without you.

Thank you also to my dad, Scott, for being available for advice on the best course of action to take and for giving me ideas to make this a success. Thank you for being there for me when I needed guidance.

A special thank you as well to Jason Collins and his team for combing through this book and making it look amazing. Your hard work has not gone unnoticed.

And to my friends – Amanda, Tally, Amber, Jean, and so many others – who took the time to either read this book or just gave me feedback and support...with all my heart, I thank you.

To Mindi Abair, if she ever picks up this book, your music got me through high school. Thank you for inspiring the title of this book and making it more than just a song. Thank you for the music you created during the time frame of this book, and continue to create. You have no idea how much your music means to me. Rock on, girlfriend!

Lastly, thank you to my husband, Cody. You stood by my side with any project I wanted to take on and cheered me on. You're the best gift I could've ever asked for. I love you more every day.

Till next time,
Sarah Blynne

ABOUT THE AUTHOR

Sarah has written stories since she was a kid growing up in Tacoma, Washington. *Bloom* is her first published work, and looks forward to publishing more. She resides in Renton, Washington with her husband and cat. In her spare time, Sarah likes to write, play video games, go on walks, drink coffee, cook, and spend time with her family, friends, and cat.